Balancing ACT

Previously in the Go-for-Gold Gymnasts series

Winning Team

THE GO-for-GOLD GYMNASTS

Balancing ACT

by DOMINIQUE MOCEANU
and ALICIA THOMPSON

DISNEP • Hyperion Books

New York

Printed in the United States of America
First Edition
10 9 8 7 6 5 4 3 2 1
J689-1817-1-12032

Library of Congress Cataloging-in-Publication Data

Moceanu, Dominique, 1981–
   Go-for-gold gymnasts: balancing act / by Dominique Moceanu and Alicia
Thompson.—1st ed.
   p. cm.—(The go-for-gold gymnasts; bk. 2)
   Summary: Twelve-year-old Noelle Onesti has everything it takes to be an elite
gymnast, as was her mother, except the money required to travel and compete
since her family's store is not doing well and their house may be going into
foreclosure.
   ISBN 978-1-4231-3632-3
   [1. Gymnastics—Fiction. 2. Friendship—Fiction. 3. Competition
(Psychology)—Fiction. 4. Family life—Texas—Fiction. 5. Houston (Tex.)—
Fiction.] I. Thompson, Alicia, 1984– II. Title.
   PZ7.M71278Gob 2012
   [Fic]—dc23   2011023747

Book design by Tyler Nevins
Text is set in 13-point Minion Pro.

Visit www.disneyhyperionbooks.com

To my mother and dearly departed father. As Romanians starting a new life in America, your courage and resolve planted the seed in my heart to become a champion. For this and countless other reasons, I will always be grateful to you.
—D.M.

For my mother, who always supported me
—A.T.

One

Ever since Mr. Van Buren had used the term *muscle memory* in science class, I'd been obsessed with the idea. The concept wasn't new to me, but now I had a name for it. I'd been doing gymnastics practically since I could walk, so it was easy to believe that there were memories buried deep in the muscles of my legs and feet that were way older than the memory of the first time I ate watermelon, or saw the ocean.

Now, standing at the very corner of the floor mat on my tiptoes, ready to launch into a tumbling pass, it wasn't like I had time to consider all of the philosophical implications of this idea. But that was the whole point of muscle memory—I didn't *have* to think. It was just there, in the flex of my ankles, the texture of the mat under the balls of my feet as I sprang into a run across the floor, the stretch of my calves as I kick-started the momentum that would carry me flipping from one end of the mat to the other. When I landed my double pike, my feet planted firmly and my hips square with my shoulders, it was like déjà vu. My body had been in this exact position so many times that I lay in bed at night and re-created it, until it was almost like I fell asleep flipping.

Cheng nodded his head and twirled his finger, his signal for *again*. With Cheng, you learned that this was all you were going to get. He was not the most vocal of coaches, and would never be the one to sweep you up in a bear hug on national television and scream, "You did it! You did it!" but he showed his satisfaction in other ways. Mostly, it was by telling you to keep working.

"Man," Britt said, rubbing chalk on the bottoms of her feet as she joined me at the corner of the floor. "Hasn't he heard of the Thirteenth Amendment? I'm pretty sure it abolished slavery."

I smiled just enough to let Britt know I'd heard

her, but not so much that it might have looked like I was participating in the conversation. Britt was the newest gymnast at Texas Twisters, and when she first got there, she had made a lot of waves because of how outspoken she was. She worked harder than she let on, and she was more determined now than she used to be, but sometimes she still joked around. It could be fun, but pretty much the only thing that scared me more than spiders was getting into trouble, so I tried not to give the coaches any reason to call me out.

Christina had been stretching on the side, but came over to line up behind Britt. "It can't be slavery if you're paying to be here," she said, rolling her eyes.

I preferred to avoid thinking about the dollars adding up and multiplying for every day that I trained at Texas Twisters. My parents never talked about how much it cost, exactly, but I knew being an Elite gymnast was not cheap.

"Noelle," Christina said, jabbing me in the shoulder, "are you going to go, or what?"

I blinked, realizing that somehow I'd allowed myself to get distracted, when that was the last thing I should have been doing as the competitive season started. Squaring myself up on a corner of the blue mat, I took another deep breath and allowed muscle memory to take over.

When we'd finished stretching at the end of practice, our coach Mo called all of us together. Adrenaline made my heart race; I knew what this would be about. The U.S. Junior National Championships were coming up in a few months—so close it was like reaching out to grab the high bar after a big release skill. I only hoped I could catch it.

Mo surveyed the four of us: me, Christina, Britt, and Jessie, who'd returned full-time to practice but wasn't planning on trying for Nationals. She'd taken some time off to cope with her eating disorder, and was still dealing with it. We had all been walking on eggshells, afraid of saying the wrong thing, but she mostly didn't talk about it.

Christina was examining her brand-new manicure as though this meeting didn't have anything to do with the most important event in her career so far. She'd just qualified for Elite competition two weeks ago, and there was no guarantee that she'd be eligible to participate in the qualifying event this early, much less in the Nationals. I could tell she was trying to act like she didn't care, but how could she not? This was *the* competition of the year, the one that determined whether or not you made the National team and got to compete internationally. They featured new up-and-comers from that competition in the biggest gymnastics magazines in the world. It was huge.

Even Britt wasn't pretending it was all a joke, the way she sometimes did. Her blue eyes were sparkling, and she was clenching and unclenching her fists at her side as though she could actually reach out and touch that National Championship gold medal. I felt a spurt of competitiveness. Nothing against Britt, but I'd be more than happy for her to take home the silver and leave the gold for me.

"You know this is important time," Mo said. Mo wasn't a talker, either, but compared to Cheng, she might as well have been Oprah. Maybe that was why Cheng was happy to spot us on the floor and help us with vault timers while Mo handled the business side of things.

"U.S. Classic is in one month," Mo continued, referring to the event that would determine whether Britt and Christina would go to Nationals. I'd already qualified earlier in the year, through a training camp. "Here, you are not against each other. You are together. Understand?"

Britt and Christina exchanged a look, but both nodded. It had been a little tense the past few months, until we decided that Britt could be just as much a friend as a threat, and I knew that Mo didn't want us to be distracted by that kind of drama as we started training for the Classic.

Only a handful of gymnasts qualified for Nationals through a training camp, and it was a relief to be one of them, since it meant that I could focus completely on that goal without worrying about the Classic. Every year, Coach Piserchia held these training camps where he invited gymnasts from all over the country to participate. This year, I'd been the only representative from Texas Twisters, and it was one of the most nerve-racking experiences of my life. Coach Piserchia was officially retired from individual coaching, but he still played a huge role in deciding who would represent our country at World Championships and at the Olympics, so impressing him was majorly important.

Now, Mo handed each of us a thick envelope. "Make sure parents get this," she said. "They need to come to meeting at gym, too."

It was irrational, since everyone had gotten an envelope, and surely *everyone* couldn't be in trouble, but like I said, I get paranoid. I hated the thought of people being mad at me, so as I looked down at the sealed envelope filled with papers intended for my parents' eyes only, all kinds of scenarios started whirling through my head. Maybe it was an assessment of my abilities up to this point, and Mo wanted to break it to them gently that any chance of my making the Olympics someday was very, very slim. Or maybe Cheng had noticed my distraction earlier that day and added it to a list of times when I'd been off my game. I mean, I thought I worked hard and did my best, but I got tired and restless just like anyone else.

"Mo?" I asked, once the other girls had moved toward the lockers.

She looked at me, not blinking as I tried to figure out how to word my question without sounding too insane. *What is in the envelope?!?!?*

"I'll probably have to read some of this stuff to my parents, since their English isn't so good," I said, and immediately felt guilty. It was true that my parents had defected from Romania before I was born; but they'd taught themselves English by watching daytime television and reading newspapers, and they were proud of the way they'd made a life for themselves here. Sometimes there were still things I needed to explain or help them with, but if it weren't for their accents they could have passed for having been born in this country.

"Okay," Mo said. "You can read to them."

"So it's not . . . secret or anything?"

"No, Noelle. It's not bad." One corner of her mouth pulled up, and I blushed. Of course she would know exactly what I was trying to get at. "It's just information about competition—boring, grown-up information, like flight to Philadelphia and leotards and money and itinerary. You don't need to worry."

The weight in my chest lifted, but only for a second, as Mo walked away, and then it settled in deeper than before. At least if I had been in trouble, I could have done something to fix it, like work harder, or apologize. But this was something I couldn't fix. Mo's words echoed in my brain—*flights, leotards, money*—and suddenly, my dream of the National Championships seemed impossible.

To go to that training camp with Coach Piserchia, my parents had had to take out a second mortgage on the building that housed both our home and our family's business. They'd made such an investment already I didn't know if I could ask them to make another one so soon. Then again, everything we'd put into gymnastics so far wouldn't have been worth much if I didn't take it all the way.

I tried to take a deep breath and visualize myself grabbing for that high bar that represented my dreams, feeling the smooth wood as I wrapped my fingers securely around the bar. But for some reason, whenever I got to that part, I could only imagine brushing it with my fingertips, close enough to leave marks in the chalk, but not close enough to stop myself from falling.

Two

As soon as I set foot in my parents' store, I knew the envelope would have to wait. There was a line of customers all the way back to the shelves with the zacuscă spread (made with eggplant or cooked beans, and one of the many things that I get weird looks for when I unpack my lunch bag), and I saw only my brother Radu working the counter.

"Where's Mihai?" I asked, tying an apron around my jeans and T-shirt. I was still wearing my leotard under that, which meant that I was now technically wearing three layers of clothes. In Texas. In June. In a store that had only a few overhead fans rattling weakly to disperse the heat.

Radu shrugged. "He was supposed to be here right after school, but I guess something came up."

"Something *always* comes up," I muttered, but pinned a smile on my face for the next customer in line. "How can I help you?"

Although we always referred to it simply as "the store," it was also a deli and bakery where we made our own dishes from scratch. We had a few regulars, mostly fellow Romanian immigrants who missed the food from their home country. Half of our usual customers were even related to us in some distant way, whether it was an aunt or an uncle or someone who had lived down the street from my parents back in Bârlad. But the woman who approached the counter was not someone I knew. She had dark, frizzy hair that looked like something out of those daytime shows my parents watched over ten years ago, and she wore more eyeliner than anyone I'd ever seen in my life.

"Oh!" she said as she approached, placing a basket of groceries on the counter. "You're so tiny I didn't even see you!"

I smiled wider, even though I get this a lot. No, I'm not quite five feet tall. Yes, I need a ladder to reach some things in the store. No, I don't need any help—I can do fifty press-to-handstand exercises straight without breaking a sweat, so I think I can manage to grab a can of pickled olives.

"Y'all are busy!" she observed, picking up one of our flyers and fanning herself with it. I was proud of those flyers. I'd made them myself with a photo editing program Mihai had illegally downloaded onto the computer, and then I'd helped my father drop them off at other local businesses and apartment complexes. *If people only knew we were here,* my father always said, *they'd come running. There's nothing like good Romanian food.*

The flyers were meant for people to take and hopefully pass along, not for someone to crinkle up in her talon fingernails as she carelessly flapped it near her face. I was glad when I finally finished ringing the woman up and was able to get through the next few customers, including a cousin and another family member whose connection I'd never been able to fully grasp.

Once the store had cleared out, I allowed myself to lean against the counter and take a breath. We had been busy, but it was temporary, I knew. We often got a small surge of people around dusk who were picking up a few things after work, but it wasn't uncommon for the store to remain completely empty for the rest of the evening. Still, we stayed open until nine o'clock every night, with my father usually wolfing down his dinner sitting on a stepladder in the storage closet, then going back to stocking shelves even as he finished chewing his last bite.

That's where I found him: in the storage closet. Mama hated it when he shut himself in there. *Let one of the boys do it,* she always said. *Their backs are younger.* But the truth was that my father was the shyest person I knew, even shyer than me, and he still got so tongue-tied dealing with customers that he preferred someone else to handle the front during the rush.

"Hey, Tata," I said, as he leaned down to press a kiss to my forehead. "Is Mama upstairs?"

"Mihai was supposed to be here so Radu could watch the twins," he said gruffly. "But he didn't show."

Mihai was the oldest, and was just finishing tenth grade; Radu was in ninth grade, and the twins, Cristian and Costel, were four. It seemed like we used to be one big happy family, with Mama and

Tata working in the store and my brothers helping, but lately Mihai had been flaking out, and Radu was starting to get resentful about working while Mihai got to do whatever he wanted. And then my younger brothers were getting to be a handful, always running around underfoot, and there I was, stuck in the middle of the whole thing. I felt guilty when I was at the gym, because I knew I could have been helping at home, and I felt trapped and restless at home, because I wanted to be at the gym.

I loved my oldest brother—he'd always been able to make me laugh, from the time I was born. My mom said I had awarded my first smile to Mihai at only two months old, when he tickled my feet. But at times like this, when I saw the lines etched in my father's face, I just wanted to shake Mihai and tell him to stop being so selfish.

"How was gym?" Tata asked. It was hard to tell if he was smiling or not underneath his bushy mustache, but I knew he was, from the crinkling around his eyes. He loved hearing about my gymnastics, even though he never really understood it. Mama had been an Elite gymnast back in Romania, so her questions were deeper, more probing, but Tata just wanted to know if I enjoyed myself and if

I still followed the same dream I had had since I was three years old.

I thought of that thick envelope, slid neatly in between my warm-up clothes and my water bottle at the bottom of my gym bag. It seemed impossible that my dream could be contained in that envelope, written on slips of paper, disguised as flight numbers and hotel arrangements.

"Oh, you know," I said, "when I was doing my giant swings on the uneven bars, I felt like I was flying!"

This was the kind of thing my father loved to hear. To him, gymnastics was an exhilarating experience, like bungee-jumping or skydiving. He'd seen the calluses on my hands and the blisters on my toes, but he prefered to pretend they didn't exist. In his mind, my feet never touched the ground.

The stillness in our upstairs apartment told me that the twins were already in bed. If they were awake, they would've immediately rushed me at the door, each vying for my attention until my mother appeared behind them, reminding them gently to take turns. Even though it was nice to have peace and quiet, I missed the usual routine.

"Mama?" I called out. I thought she was probably watching television in the room she shared with my father and the twins. After all those years of watching daytime soap operas, my mother's one true addiction was television. Lately, she'd been watching all of these embarrassing reality shows about rich kids hooking up, going to parties, and getting into trouble. It was weird to hear my mother talk about the same program all the kids at school were watching, too.

I knocked softly before pushing her door open, expecting to find her sitting in the rocking chair, folding laundry while she watched the latest episode. She'd always look up from the clothes when something got really juicy or good, which meant that she only made it through one basket per show, and she'd make this clicking sound with her tongue whenever a character did something she disapproved of. Which, of course, was often.

But she wasn't sitting in her chair. Instead, I found her sprawled out on the bed, still wearing her glasses, a pile of papers strewn next to her. There was a thin line of drool hanging from one corner of her mouth, and she was snoring.

Her favorite show was playing softly in the

background; I switched it off. Those kids who went out all night and did whatever they liked would probably have been mortified to find a parent looking like this—clothes rumpled, no makeup on. Even without all those cameras, even if no one else in the world would ever have had to see, they'd probably have been disgusted that their parents could show any sign that they weren't perfect.

But it just made me sad. There was a pile of envelopes next to my sleeping mother, including one from the gas company, with a red outline around the dollar amount that let us know our payment was late again, and one from the insurance company, on pink paper that told us our rates were going up. And I thought about my own envelope from gym, and wondered how I could ever think it contained my dream. All it contained was another bill.

The last couple of weeks of school were always crazy, and most teachers didn't even bother trying to teach anything. But Mr. Van Buren had to be different, and so he was talking about muscle fatigue and pretending to ignore everyone passing notes and giggling in the back of the class.

I never passed notes. Yet another symptom of

being the girl who stays out of trouble, but also . . . it wasn't like I had anyone to pass them to. My only real friends at school were Christina and Jessie, and I saw them at lunch, and that was it. I had nothing against my classmates, but when you spend most of your waking time outside of school at the gym, it makes it hard to bond with girls over sleepovers or trips to the mall.

"What is muscle fatigue?" Mr. Van Buren asked the class expectantly. He had just gone over the definition half an hour ago, and so it should have been an easy one. But it's like that riddle he'd told us once: if a teacher talks during the last week of school, does he still make a sound? Nobody was paying attention.

Tentatively, I raised my hand, and Mr. Van Buren beamed at me. "Yes, Noelle."

"Muscle fatigue is when you can't perform normal movements, or when it requires more effort than it should to perform normal movements."

"Exactly, Noelle!" One thing I would miss about Mr. Van Buren was that he always acted like you'd just said something brilliant, even when you were only parroting something he'd said earlier in the class. I felt myself flush, and I only got redder as I listened to the whispering behind me.

"Like *she* ever has muscle fatigue," one girl said.

"Oh, I know. Have you seen her arms? She looks like a comic-book character."

"And *not* in a good way," the first girl added.

Self-consciously, I tried to hide my upper arms with my hands, feeling the familiar ripple of muscle underneath my T-shirt. Normally, I was proud of my strength and what I could do with it. But sometimes, like when I was forced to wear a junior bridesmaid's dress with spaghetti straps for my cousin's wedding, I felt like a big freak. All of the other girls had looked like little princesses, whereas I looked . . . well, like I was about to run down the vault runway and attack it wearing pink tulle.

I was relieved when the bell finally rang and I could go meet Christina and Jessie at lunch. Britt was homeschooled, which was too bad, because she was really smart, and it would've been nice to have a friendly face in my advanced science class.

If I felt out of place during my classes, it all changed when I sat with Christina and Jessie. Maybe it was because we'd been so worried about Jessie lately that it made my problems seem petty by comparison. Or maybe it was because Christina was so beautiful and confident, and some of that rubbed off on me when I was sitting next to her. If Christina had heard those girls whispering about *her*, she probably would've turned around and flexed her bicep and then said something about using it to punch their lights out, or something cutting about how they *wished* they looked like Wonder Woman.

"Can you believe Ms. Rizzi passed out bags of candy, like we were in kindergarten?" Christina was saying when I sat down. "How lame."

I saw the moment when Christina actually reflected on the words coming out of her mouth. Her face got a pinched look, and she glanced nervously at Jessie. "I mean, candy is cool and all—" she started to say, but Jessie held up her hand to cut her off.

"How many times do I have to tell you? It's okay to talk about food. You're supposed to talk about food! Look, I brought a healthy lunch, and I plan on eating it. Okay?"

Christina was still a little pale as she bit into her chicken salad, and it occurred to me that even she wasn't completely immune to self-doubt. But then she flipped her hair and gave a flirtatious smile to a guy at another table, and I figured I must've imagined any chink in her armor.

"I am *so* excited about the end-of-year dance," she said. "Do you think Logan will ask me?"

Jessie shrugged, but there was a glint in her eye. "I heard that Kelly was asking about you."

"No! Really?" Christina made a face. "He's so *gross*. And hello, Kelly is a girl's name. Didn't anyone give his mom a baby-name book?"

"Kelly can be a boy's name," I pointed out. "I think it's cool that someone likes you. I don't think anyone's ever liked me."

Christina rolled her eyes. "Whatever. You're so cute, you're like a little doll, with your brown hair and your big brown eyes. Who are you going to go to the dance with?"

I took a loud, crunchy bite of a carrot stick to avoid answering the question, but when I was done chewing, both Jessie and Christina were still staring at me, obviously expecting me to answer. "I didn't think we were allowed to go," I said finally.

"What do you mean, *allowed*?" Christina asked.

I glanced back and forth between the two of them in disbelief. "Competition season is starting! Once school is out, we're going to be training eight hours a day. There's no time for dances."

Jessie sighed. "I probably wasn't going to go, anyway," she said. "It's not like I've been asked."

"No, we're going." Christina slammed the palm of her hand against the table with such force that some of my lite ranch dressing splattered onto my shirt. "Forget the boys, we're going together. And forget gym! We can have our full practice on Friday, still have time for frozen yogurt afterward, and show up at the dance fashionably late."

Christina saw the look on my face. "Don't worry, Cinderella, we'll get you home before you turn into a pumpkin. And the experience will leave you energized, ready to take on Nationals!"

Nationals, the dance . . . these were the last things I wanted to think about at this point. Trying to figure out what to do about one led to worrying about the other, and it was too much. I reached for a napkin and started dabbing at the spots on my shirt while Jessie and Christina talked about dresses and hairstyles. At least ranch dressing was something I could clean up . . . unlike the rest of my life.

Three

It was true that I was worried about the dance being off limits. After all, there was a reason Christina wasn't asking Mo about it. It was also true that I didn't have a dress, couldn't afford a dress, and looked like a stupid munchkin in dresses anyway. But there was one thing I hadn't shared with Christina and Jessie, another reason I wasn't looking forward to the dance, and that reason was standing over by the pommel horse.

Scott Pattison. With his dark, curly hair and blue eyes, he'd have been reason enough to come to the gym, even if I didn't care about someday winning an Olympic gold medal. So what if he was eighteen and about to start college and had barely said five words to me except for the time he'd tried to help find my stuffed animal (it was a good-luck charm, but still, embarrassing). So what that he already drove a car and probably had a girlfriend who was taller than a midget, but not so tall she'd tower over him? And I bet she wasn't a gymnast, which meant she could actually have a body that looked good in prom dresses. Whenever I was in the gym, I couldn't help sneaking little looks at him as he flipped across the floor or wiped his brow with a towel.

And let's face it: it would have been ridiculous for a twelve-year-old girl to ask a guy like that to a school dance, much less for him to say yes. Even if he did come, he'd probably be doing it for community service hours for college. *Chaperoned middle-school dance. Made some girl's dream come true.*

Britt caught me staring. I blinked quickly. "Chalk in my eye," I said.

"Uh-huh."

It occurred to me that Britt might actually be the perfect person to talk to, given that she didn't go to our school. "It's just that—" I began, waiting for Jessie to pass by before continuing, "there's this dance at our school in a week."

"And you want to go with *Scott*?" Britt blurted out. "He's, like, ancient. You'd be slow-dancing and you'd hear his bones creak."

Now I remembered why it was a bad idea to tell Britt anything. It wasn't so much that she was terrible at keeping secrets as that she had no concept that you might not want everything shouted across the gym through a megaphone (which was about the volume of her everyday speaking voice).

"I didn't say anything about Scott," I snapped. "I was just thinking about this dance, that's all. Christina and Jessie really want to go, but I'm not sure. . . . Don't you think it'll interfere with training?"

"Probably."

It was the honest answer I was expecting, so there was no explanation for the fact that I suddenly felt deflated. "Of course it will," I said. "I'll be off all through practice, because I'll be thinking about it, and then I'll be tired the next day, because I'll have been out too late. Plus, I haven't even mentioned it to my parents, and who knows what Mo would say?"

Britt clapped her hands together, sending the freshly applied chalk flying into the air. Now I really did have chalk in my eye.

"So, don't ask permission," Britt said. "Better to ask forgiveness, right?"

That was my anti-motto. I always asked permission, and I hated the uncertainty of asking someone to forgive me for something I'd already done.

"Are you saying I should go, or not?" At that point, I really just wanted a concrete answer; it was like Britt was the devil or the angel on my shoulder, and I would have to do whatever she said.

Britt turned to me. "Yes, it might cause a blip in your training routine. But yes, you should go. How many times do you get to do something fun like that? Some of us don't even have school dances to go to."

Now I felt bad. I hadn't even considered that Britt might be jealous, or feel left out. "You could probably come," I said. "Nobody would have to—"

"Don't worry about it," Britt cut in. "I'll just spend another rip-roaring evening at home with my grandmother, learning about the Battle of 1812 or whatever other random thing she wants to talk about at the dinner table, as though I didn't just hear about it *all day*. That's where you're really lucky to be in public school: your parents probably don't quiz you on multiplication tables on weekends just because they're around and can't think of anything else to do."

That was true. My parents rarely asked me about school—both because I'd always gotten good grades and because they were too busy to really think about it. Just like how, lately, they'd been too preoccupied to do anything about the fact that Mihai was out with his friends more than he was at home, and just last week I accidentally put one of his shirts in my load of laundry and noticed it smelled like smoke.

"So . . . you're giving a thumbs-up to the dance?" I said. I knew I was being neurotic, but like I said, I'm a worrier. I needed someone's absolute conviction to persuade me, and even then I knew that I'd go home and second-guess myself.

Britt sighed. She was familiar enough with my flaws by now to know exactly what I was doing. "You know that song by the Clash?" she said, without bothering to look at me. I shook my head. Another of my flaws: I was hopeless with pop culture. "'Should I Stay or Should I Go?' The answer, Noelle, is *always* go."

I wrinkled my forehead. "Why's that?" I could think of lots of times it might have been better to stay home. Like if my family was taking another trip to the circus, which had been our big present one Christmas but which I had hated every second of. The clowns were scary, the animals were sad, and the whole place smelled weird.

"Isn't it obvious? Wherever you could go, it's probably better than where you are. And between staying home on a Friday night and going out with your friends . . . well, that's a no-brainer."

Mo walked by, her gaze sharp as she looked at us. "Enough chalk," she said. "Britt, work on your giants reps on the strap bar. Noelle, you go with Cheng to work on your release."

"Sorry," I muttered, my head down.

Britt's apology was chirpier, almost cheerful. Then she leaned in toward me. "See? If we had asked permission for that conversation, Mo would've said no, and we never would've had it. But now, we got to chat, we said we were sorry, and we're about to continue our workout. No harm, no foul."

I remembered the way Mo's face had looked in that instant, her mouth tight with disapproval, and I wondered how Britt could say that. Even if I was the recipient of that look for only five seconds, I would dwell on it for the next five days. At least, if

I asked permission, I didn't have that sinking feeling in my gut.

One thing people may not realize about gymnastics: even when you land on mats, it still stings a bit. Not as much as it would if we were practicing on hard wooden floors, like they did in the olden days, but think about your body being propelled through the air and then stopping suddenly as your feet smack onto a mat that's designed to be soft, but firm. Sometimes we practice new or risky skills into a pit filled with foam, and that's a blast, but when we're just landing dismounts onto the regular mats in practice, it can start taking its toll on the ankles.

I had landed my sixth double tuck in a row when Mo approached me. Immediately, I worried that I'd been cowboying my legs too much—which meant not keeping my knees together—or that I was piking down as I hit the mat, which would cost me valuable tenths of a point in competition if I had to take a step on the landing to keep my balance. I waited for Mo to say something about my form or technique, but instead she just pursed her lips and looked at me as though sizing me up.

"Yes," she said, even though I hadn't spoken. "You need to add full twist to dismount. Only way to be competitive."

I'd been wanting to add a full-twisting double back to my routine for forever. But I wasn't like Britt, who could just toss out a new move and have faith that her coach would let her do what she wanted. I thought about each new skill for a while, visualized myself successfully completing it, and then hoped that my coaches could read my mind and would let me increase my difficulty level.

"Okay," I said. "I mean, great. I'm ready."

Mo nodded. "With full twist, you make National team."

Even though Mo was more talkative than Cheng, she didn't say any more than she needed to, and she didn't often give praise. Encouragement, maybe, but not outright praise. This was even better—Mo was telling me straight up that I would make the National team. Not that I would do my best, or that I would try, but that I would definitely make it.

I wanted to jump up on the beam and throw a high, tight, full-twisting double-tuck dismount of Guinness World Records proportions, but I knew I

30

had to be patient and wait. It was just so hard when I felt as if I could already fly.

"Your parents will be able to be at meeting next Friday night, yes?" Mo asked.

My stomach plummeted with the same force as those dismounts I'd been landing earlier. There was already reason to dread the meeting with the huge dollar sign attached to it, but next Friday was also the night of the dance. How would we get away with going to a dance when our parents would all be at the gym that very same night, listening to speeches about how focused we needed to be right now?

I thought of that song that Britt had mentioned, but I knew that the differences between me and Britt were greater than just our knowledge of music. While she wouldn't have thought twice about hounding the coaches until they let her compete a new skill, I figured that, when it came to my skills, they knew best, and I held my tongue until they thought I was ready. While her motto might have been always to choose *go*, I pretty much always stayed.

That night, I tried really hard to give the envelope to my mother. I caught her at the best time, when she'd put the twins to bed and before she'd completely shut down for the night.

"Can I help you, Mama?" I asked, reaching for a rag to dry the dishes she was washing and placing in the rack.

"Don't you have homework?"

I shook my head. "It's the last few weeks of school. I think the teachers have given up."

She smiled, handing me a handful of forks and knives she'd just run under the faucet. "How is gym? You know, I've been meaning to come see you, but with watching the boys and running the store . . ."

"I know," I said, and I really did. Of course, I loved it when my family came to see me practice, even when my mother or father came alone or with the twins. And they never missed a competition. But with my parents the only full-time employees of the store, it was hard for them to get away. Half the time, my mother brought the boys downstairs with her and had them count out beans while she worked. It was amazing to me how long she could keep them going on the bean-counting game. Maybe she'd done the same with me when I was little, and that was why I actually understood and liked math.

"I'll be training most of the summer," I said,

"but we still get Sundays off, and a half day on Wednesdays, so I could help around the store if you needed me to."

"You," my mom said, leaning over to kiss my cheek, "are so sweet. But you work too hard as it is, and you know you shouldn't be in the store. You're only twelve."

"I can do everything Radu can," I protested. "Even carrying boxes—I'm stronger than him, you know." This was a sore point between my brother and me, ever since I'd beat him at arm-wrestling last Christmas in front of all our cousins. I could probably have beaten Mihai, too, but he never let himself lose. He always found a way to make a joke of things he wasn't good at, so people thought he was playing around.

"You'd be employee of the year," my mother assured me, "but you're too young. I don't want you spending all of your time in the store when you have school and gymnastics, and besides, there are laws."

My father had worked in my grandfather's store from the age of five, sorting things in the back, and he believed that the only way to teach children a work ethic was to start them young in the family business. But my mother was more cautious. She was very conscious of the fact that we'd come over to this country to pursue opportunities we wouldn't have had in Romania, and she didn't want to do anything to mess that up. She wouldn't even go a mile over the speed limit. If she had known that I'd worked behind the counter the other day, she'd have gotten that worry line between her eyes and told me to not even think about tying an apron on again. Assisting my father in the stockroom was sometimes okay, or organizing shelves when no one was in the store, but interacting with customers was a definite no-no.

"Enough talk about work," my mother said. "What about play? What things have you girls cooked up for the summer? I'm sure Mrs. Flores will take you all to the carnival again. You had so much fun last year."

This was the perfect opportunity to bring up the dance, and then lead in to the competition. I could say, *Actually, there's this big dance at school,* and I knew my mother would be excited and would start planning to sew me a dress to wear. Then I could say, *I'm just worried it will interfere with training. Remember, Mama, that this is the first summer I might be eligible for the Junior National team. And* she'd say, *Oh, no, you have to go to the dance! And don't you worry about Nationals. Your father and I have been saving for it for the past year, and you're going to do so great that you deserve a night off.*

It was all complete fantasy, of course. My mother would offer to sew me a dress for the dance if I wanted, although she'd express a little concern about its distracting me from my training. She liked to see me enjoy myself, but she'd been an Elite gymnast, too, and she knew what even the slightest hiccup in routine could mean for an athlete. And that big red square around the amount due on the gas bill meant that my parents probably hadn't been saving up money to send me to Philadelphia for Nationals. Not that I could blame them—they already spent almost as much on my training as they did on the mortgage for the store.

So I decided to ignore the rest of my mother's questions and just focus on the easy one. "Yeah, I think Christina mentioned something about her mom taking us all to the carnival when it comes to town." That would be in late June, and the Classic wasn't until the end of July, so hopefully it would work out. I kept that part to myself. "I love those Elephant Ears!"

I thought for sure my mother would know something was up then. I mean, Elephant Ears are good and all, but I usually only eat a few bites of one, since it's nothing but fried carbs and sugar . . . not exactly the staples of an athlete's diet. I also cringed when I imagined how I must have sounded. *I love those Elephant Ears*? Was that really the best I could come up with?

But I guess my mother didn't notice my bizarre enthusiasm, because she just smiled. "I used to love the corn dogs," she said. "When we first came to America, we couldn't believe that they even existed. What was a hot dog? And what was this hot dog on a stick with the bread already wrapped around it?"

I laughed weakly. Even though I desperately wanted to mention the envelope and the parents' meeting and just get it all out there, I was also relieved to be talking about something as unthreatening as fried carnival foods.

My mother finished rinsing the last plate and handed it to me to dry, switching the faucet off and wiping her hands on her skirt in a gesture that was very familiar to me. She didn't care what she wore or if she was covered in baby spitup or flour from baking, so long as the store was running smoothly and her children were happy.

"Well," she said. "You let me know when you go, and I'm sure we can spare twenty dollars for you to make yourself sick on Elephant Ears."

And that's the real reason the envelope stayed in my nightstand drawer upstairs. It wasn't that I was scared of my mother's telling me we didn't have the money for me to go. It was that I was scared to think what she might sacrifice to make sure that I got what I wanted.

Four

That night, I couldn't sleep, so I was still awake at midnight when the front door creaked open. For a few moments, I just lay there, my muscles still and my eyes wide as I stared at the ceiling.

Someone's robbed the store, I thought. Now there's definitely no way we can afford that trip to Philadelphia for Nationals.

I didn't have time to feel guilty about that selfish thought before it occurred to me that I might not even *make* it to Nationals if someone came in and murdered me in my sleep. The newspaper would run a story around the time I would've been going to the competition, about the local girl whose life was cruelly cut short before her potential could be realized. Christina would go to Nationals, and she'd wear a black leotard or some kind of armband as a tribute to her fallen teammate, and she'd tearfully dedicate her gold medal to me (well, maybe not tearfully—even in my fantasy, it was hard to imagine her crying).

Then I thought about my little brothers, lying all sweaty and intertwined in the bed they shared, and my mother and father, sleeping soundly after a hard day's work. As much as I wanted to dive under the bed and hide, I wondered if I could just warn my parents before anything bad happened. I pictured myself saving the day; maybe the police department would give me some kind of reward, which I could use to pay my own way to Philadelphia. It was completely ridiculous, but at least it calmed me down.

I slipped out of bed, wishing I was wearing more than a tank top and shorts that spelled out GYM RAT across my butt. When I stubbed my toe on the corner of my dresser, I bit my lip to stop myself from crying out, and then I edged out of my bedroom, trying to make myself as small as possible. Sometimes there were benefits to being so short.

If I had come across any robbers or would-be killers, I would've distracted them by doing a back walkover and then kicking them in the crotch or something, but it turned out not to be necessary. The only person I surprised was my brother Mihai, and he jumped even higher than I did. He almost stepped into the pot my parents had placed on the ground next to the couch, which had a quarter inch of rainwater in it from where the roof leaked above.

"What are you doing up?" he hissed, once he'd finally stopped huffing and puffing. Now that the danger of a break-in was past, I was enjoying seeing my brother caught off guard.

"What are you doing sneaking in?" I shot back.

He waved his hand towards my parents' closed door. "Keep your voice down," he said. "And mind your own business."

I could do the first thing, but not the second. "Where have you been?"

Mihai ran his hand through his dark hair. "I ran downstairs to get something to eat, okay? Are you satisfied, Snoopy McSnoop?"

Maybe it was just because I hadn't seen him for more than a few minutes here and there in the past couple of weeks, but suddenly he looked taller, and

I noticed that he had a couple of angry red blotches on his chin. It was weird to think of my brother having acne and those strange raised veins in his arms the way older guys did, but there was the evidence, right in front of my face. My brother had changed, and not just physically—gone was the guy who used to make me laugh by pretending to be a Southern belle or a talk-show host, and in his place was this guy who disappeared in the middle of the night and lied about it. I knew he hadn't just gone downstairs—for one thing, we had more than enough food in the kitchen, and for another, we never helped ourselves to stuff from the store without asking my parents. Somehow I knew that even if my brother broke curfew and all kinds of other rules, he would never have broken that one.

I could tell from the way his gaze met mine that his thoughts were running along the same lines. Wherever he was coming back from, it must have been bad if he'd rather have had me think he was taking food from the store without permission.

"Please, tell me," I said. "I won't say anything, I promise."

If there was anyone Mihai could trust, he had to know it was me. When he and Radu broke our great-grandmother's vase, I'd kept my mouth shut. They'd glued it back together and turned it so that the cracked side faced the wall, and I hadn't said a word when Mama was dusting one day and it just fell apart.

Mihai rolled his eyes, but then he admitted, "I hung out with some friends. That's it. Maybe you'd get it if you did anything besides school and gymnastics."

In all the years I'd been doing gymnastics, I don't think I'd ever heard my brothers complain, even though they had to resent certain things. While they had to share a secondhand gaming system, I got a new leotard and some hair ties. They had been dragged to Saturday competitions and forced to sit through endless presentations of awards, though I knew they'd rather have been out with their friends. Once, Mihai had even taped over a BMX event he'd recorded for himself when the Goodwill Games were on TV and I would've missed it otherwise.

So, while I knew Mihai had a point, it still stung to hear him say it so harshly. I wanted to tell him that he *had* a life, and that it used to include us. I wanted to tell him that I didn't think he should be hanging out with his so-called friends if they were the reason his grades were slipping and his breath smelled like an ashtray. But instead I just shrugged, like I didn't care.

"I promised I wouldn't say anything, and I won't," I said. "But you should think twice about this sneaking-around stuff."

"Mama and Tata have no clue," he said. "They're so tired at the end of the day I doubt a hurricane would wake them up." He tousled my hair in a patronizing gesture and disappeared into the bedroom he shared with Radu. It was true that my parents, although they had been concerned about Mihai's behavior lately, would probably have let him get away with it, just because of how busy they were. But that wasn't what I was trying to tell him. I was trying to warn him about thinking only of himself and not anyone else.

Then again, it wasn't like I was one to talk. My first thought, when I'd worried that someone was breaking into the store, had been about Nationals, and though I could tell that my mother had been preoccupied earlier that night, I'd been too wrapped up in my own troubles to concern myself with hers. At this point, I wasn't really sure if I was that much better than my brother.

* * *

We were waiting for Christina's mom to pick us up after school when Christina waved her hand in front of my face. "Earth to Noelle," she said. "Aren't you listening?"

I had been dwelling on the run-in last night with my brother, but I didn't want to mention that to Christina, for several reasons. For one thing, it seemed like it was getting into my family's business, and even though Christina was my best friend, I wasn't sure I wanted to tell her about all of the tension and stress at home. For another thing, sometimes I got the impression that Christina thought Mihai was cute, which was just gross.

"Sorry," I said. "I'm paying attention now, I promise."

Normally, in situations like this, Christina would have gotten huffy and refused to continue, making me apologize over and over again and then acting like it was my great privilege to listen to what she had to say. But this time, she must've been overly excited, because she launched right into her topic without even a sigh about having to start over.

"My mom bought me some glittery yellow

eye shadow," she said. "I can't wait to wear it at the dance."

"Is your dress yellow?" I asked. I hadn't even thought Christina had bought a new dress yet. I'd been to her house many times and could vouch for the fact that she had millions of dresses, all hanging up in her closet, on plastic hangers, not wire ones, because Mrs. Flores thought they got misshapen and stretched out the clothes. But this was an occasion, and there was no way Christina wasn't taking advantage of the opportunity to buy a new dress.

"Not exactly," she said. "But if the perfect dress doesn't match the eye shadow, I'll trade it in for a different color. The makeup, I mean. I only picked yellow because I read in a magazine that it was on trend for this year to wear bright colors."

I never paid attention to that kind of stuff, because . . . well, it didn't really matter to me. But sometimes I wondered whether, if I'd been given everything, the way Christina had been, maybe I'd have cared more about clothes and makeup and hair. And then maybe I'd have been more confident and outspoken, like she was, and not so afraid to stand out.

"You can totally borrow it," Christina said.

She studied my face as though she were planning my makeover in her head at that very moment. "Actually, it might be better if I exchanged it for another color, like aqua. That's still bright, and it would look nice against your complexion. Your skin is too light for yellow, I think."

"It's your makeup," I said. "You can get whichever kind you want."

Christina shrugged. "We could always ask my mom if she'd buy both."

I knew that Mrs. Flores got her makeup from one of the most expensive stores in the mall—and not just a counter in a department store, or a kiosk in the center, but an entire store devoted to lip stain and foundation and anything you could think of. She said that her skin was allergic to the cheaper stuff. I also knew that she bought Christina makeup from the same place, even though Christina had perfect skin and had probably never had a pimple in her life.

I felt my usual jealousy rise up in my throat, and it was hard for me to reply. So, instead, I just nodded.

"Your eyes are so pretty," Christina said. "We should definitely make them pop for the dance."

I grimaced. "I don't know that I want them to *pop*."

"Oh, be quiet," Christina said, laughing. "You know what I meant."

I did. And that was one of the reasons it was hard to stay mad at Christina when she brought up buying a hundred dollars' worth of makeup like it was buying a pack of gum at the gas station—she was so generous. Yes, her parents gave her whatever she wanted, but she'd always been willing to share. Over the years, she'd lent or given me countless things, and she'd never demanded them back or made me feel guilty about taking them. She would say things like, "Oh, my mom gave me this dress but I hate it, so if you could take it off my hands, that would be amazing." And I would wonder if she was just being nice or if she knew more than she let on about my family's situation. I was normally careful not to talk a lot about my home life or how the store was doing, but Christina was my best friend. In some ways, she knew me better than I knew myself.

When Mrs. Flores dropped me and Christina off at the gym after school, there was a News Channel 8 van outside. Immediately, Christina flipped down the passenger visor mirror and started smoothing her hair. "How do I look?" she asked, checking her makeup.

Once Mrs. Flores had parked the car, she licked her finger and reached over to wipe a smudge from under Christina's eye.

"Mom!" Christina protested, but she was obviously more worried about looking good on camera than about being embarrassed, so she didn't pull away. I wanted to do something about my appearance, too—after my day at school, there were probably little flyaway hairs coming out of my ponytail, and my face would have been shiny from the heat—but there was no mirror in the backseat. Besides, they'd probably end up interviewing Britt or Christina instead, anyway. Last year I'd had a small article in the paper when I was state beam champion. Britt was so outgoing, though, and Christina was so pretty that they'd made better on-camera interviewees. I'd end up stammering or whispering something stupid about how I wanted to do my best or how I knew my competition would be tough. Which was true, but, you know, hardly a scintillating sound bite.

Christina must've been worried about someone

else beating her to the interview, because she was almost running to open the front door of the gym. I tried not to be annoyed when she let it close almost in my face, and I slipped in right before Mrs. Flores, who was a little slower, because she had heels on. But when we got into the gym, it wasn't Britt they were interviewing, or even Jessie or Mo or Cheng—it was Scott. He was looking cuter than ever in a Conner University T-shirt over his usual workout clothes, and he smiled at the news reporter as she held the microphone in front of his face.

They were standing over by the big sign at the entrance—where, if they moved a little to the left, people would see HOME OF STATE BEAM CHAMPION NOELLE ONESTI underneath the Texas Twisters logo—and we could hear everything.

"It's truly a blessing," he was saying. "To be able to compete for Conner at all is amazing, but to get the scholarship on top of that . . . I know my family has worked really hard to get me where I am today, so it's nice to be able to pay them back by earning my way through school."

I melted a little bit; I couldn't have said it better myself. Clearly, Scott was perfect for me.

The interviewer beamed her approval. It was

a good thing she was, like, forty years old, or I might've been jealous. "Well, I know I speak for all of Austin when I say how proud we are. What's next for you?"

"Just training for the fall," he said. "And maybe going to the National Championships this summer. The qualifier's coming up, so wish me luck."

"Good luck!" the interviewer said, as though Scott needed it, and then did her wrap-up spiel, after which the cameraman gathered his equipment and headed toward the door. She took a moment to shake Scott's hand and say something inaudible before following. I was surprised when Christina reached out to grab the reporter's sleeve.

"Hi!" Christina said, flashing her teeth in her biggest smile. "My name is Christina Flores, and I'm one of the Junior Elite gymnasts here at Texas Twisters. I was just wondering if you wanted to talk to me, maybe, about training here? I hope to go to the Nationals this summer, too."

"Oh, good for you!" the reporter gushed. I recognized her now from television; she was the one who always wore a gold chain around her neck with a ring on it. It was surreal to see that same necklace now, up close and personal. She also wore a lot of makeup, which hadn't been as obvious on TV. With all the lights and cameras and everything, she appeared normal, but when she stood just a few feet away, it was obvious that there was a layer of foundation caked on her skin. Maybe it was better that my mother didn't let me wear makeup, if only to keep me from ever looking like that.

"Well, congratulations, and good luck!" the reporter said to Christina, smiling at me before sliding her sunglasses down over her eyes. And just like that, the reporter and the cameraman were gone.

Christina gaped after them. "I cannot *believe* that," she said. "What universe are we in where a guy gymnast is getting all the press?"

It was true that, generally, women's gymnastics was the really popular sport. Men's gymnastics got shown on TV less, had lower ratings, and didn't bring the sponsorships or publicity that women's gymnastics did. Normally I thought this was pretty unfair, but I admit that I was as stunned as Christina. Obviously, *I* knew that Scott was amazing, but why was he getting all this attention?

Mo walked by, and Christina asked her that very question.

"You don't need interview," Mo said. "You need

practice. Get changed, and get out on floor."

I hadn't really expected any other reaction from Mo, but I still made a sympathetic face at Christina as we headed toward the locker room. "It was just a question," she grumbled, although I knew she wasn't really surprised, either. Whenever the younger gymnasts were over on the floor playing a game or there was some kind of drama up at the front desk, Mo was the one to snap at us to get back to work and mind our own business.

It was a lot like how Mihai had told me to mind my own business last night. Apparently, this was a theme in my life, a huge neon sign telling me that I needed to concentrate and not let so many other things filter through.

That didn't stop me from listening when I heard Jessie explain more about the interview, of course. She'd gotten to the gym before us, and so she filled us in on a little background while we sifted through our bags for everything we needed for the day's practice. It didn't count as breaking my focus, since I hadn't even started training yet.

"The woman called it a 'human interest piece,'" Jessie said, her green eyes intent on a point on the ceiling as though she was trying to remember the reporter's exact words. "It's only because of Scott's scholarship and all that."

"Well, we're *humans*," Christina said. "Isn't Miss News Channel Eight interested in *us*?"

"But Scott found out about the scholarship a couple of months ago," I pointed out. It had been a Friday, to be exact, and he'd come in waving a folded piece of paper and had talked excitedly to Mo, who'd actually given him a hug. Hugs were even rarer than praise in Mo's world. I remembered it had been a Friday, because he'd been wearing his Birchbark High School senior class T-shirt, which is what he always wore on Fridays, to show his school spirit. That was just the kind of guy Scott was.

Jessie shrugged. "I guess he hadn't officially accepted the offer and everything until this week."

Britt came in just in time to catch the end of the conversation; she swung her locker open, and the metal clanged loudly against the locker next to it. I winced. "Are you guys talking about that interview, too?" she said. "It's all they'll talk about at the front desk. Who cares? That woman from Channel Eight is scary. Her eyelashes look like spiders' legs."

If only Britt had seen her in person. The makeup was ten times as intense.

On my way out of the locker room, I saw Scott by the water fountain, and before I could stop myself, I'd turned and was walking in his direction. He was still leaning over to get a drink when I came up behind him; I stared at the darker gray triangle that his sweat had made on the back of his shirt while I waited. If there was a picture definition of *pathetic* in the dictionary, it'd probably have been me at that moment. I mean, his sweat? I must have been crazy.

He almost jabbed me with his elbow as he spun around, wiping his mouth, and then he smiled. "Sorry," he said. There was a drop of water on the tip of his nose where he'd dipped it into the stream, and I knew if I didn't stop staring I'd make it into the thesaurus, too, for all the synonyms of *pathetic.*

"Hey," I said. "I mean, it's okay."

He started to leave, but I cleared my throat. "Cool interview," I said. I tried to make it sound casual, but my voice came out a little squeaky. "About the scholarship. That's so . . . cool."

Now I was repeating myself. I should just fill up my water bottle, I thought, and end this nightmare.

But he smiled wider, and it looked so genuine I couldn't help grinning back. "Thanks," he said.

"I'm really excited. You'll be at Birchbark next year, right?"

I couldn't believe he knew something about me! Well, almost. "The year after that," I said. "I'm only in seventh grade now."

Why had I said it like that? *Only* in seventh grade. I was too young for him, but still, there was no reason to make it so obvious. I should've said it breezily, like, *Oh, I'm going into eighth grade,* or maybe, *I wish! I still have another year of middle school to go. Kids there are so immature.*

"Awesome," he said. This was how I knew he was being nice to me, because there was nothing awesome about being in seventh grade.

"So you'll be at Nationals?" I asked. I hoped that I didn't sound as if I'd been listening too closely to his interview, even though I knew I'd probably go home and watch it that night on TV and memorize every word.

He glanced toward the parallel bars. I was probably keeping him from practice. I was keeping *myself* from practice, but this was the longest conversation I'd ever had with Scott, and I didn't want it to end.

"Hopefully," he said. "What about you? What

am I saying?—of course you'll be there. You're like some sort of prodigy."

I blushed even harder, if possible, than I already had been. Scott watched my gymnastics! And he thought I was good—a *prodigy*, even. "Well . . ." I began, wanting to sound humble, but then I couldn't think of anything to say. The word hung in the air for an awkward moment before Scott raised his eyebrows.

"So, I'll see you there," he said. "Have a good practice today."

"You've been to Nationals before, right?" I blurted out. Out of the corner of my eye, I could see the other girls stretching on the floor, and I fumbled for my water bottle. Just a few more seconds, I told myself, and then I'll get back to work.

"Yeah, I went two years ago, but last year . . . You might remember, I pulled a hamstring."

He'd been doing a really cool flare on the pommel horse at the time, and all of a sudden I'd glanced over and he was on the ground, holding his leg. It had taken him a couple of weeks to get back to his full strength, and in the meantime, he'd missed his chance to qualify.

"What's it like?" I asked. "It's just that I've

never been before, and I'm a little nervous."

Did he think I was flirting with him? My voice sounded all weird and breathless to me, and I didn't want him to think I was coming on to him, even though I kind of was. Then again, I thought guys liked it when girls flirted, so maybe it was okay if he thought that was what I was doing. I was feeling lightheaded, and I hadn't even started flying around the uneven bars yet.

"It's fun," he said. "I mean, it's a lot of pressure, but you'll do fine. Just treat it like any other meet. Listen, I have to get back to training, but if you have any other questions about Nationals, just let me know. Okay?"

I nodded and watched him walk away. Had that gone well? I wished I could tell. He'd been in a rush to get away from me, which was not really a good sign. But then again, he'd invited me to talk to him again, so that meant a door had opened at least a little bit to a future interaction. And of course he'd wanted to get back to training—that was what I liked most about him. He was totally dedicated to gymnastics, and he knew what was important.

It only reminded me that, while Scott was showing his true work ethic, I was standing there at the water fountain as my teammates warmed up. I hurried to fill up my bottle, splashing a little in my rush to finish and get out there on the floor.

"What was that all about?" Christina whispered when I finally took my place, but I shook my head, not wanting to get into trouble with Mo for talking. I was just relieved that my face was pressed against my knees as I reached for my toes, and she couldn't see the silly smile that I was finding it hard to suppress.

Five

Sunday was the only day in the week we got off practice, unless it was Christmas or some other major holiday, and those Sundays were supposed to help make up for all the "family time" we missed out on throughout the week. Usually, I spent my family time working in the store, which I guess counted.

We stayed open most Sunday mornings in case a customer came by, but it was generally slow until lunchtime. So, when the door to the store swung open, my mother and I both looked up, surprised. My mother greeted the newcomer with a smile.

"Good morning," she said.

"Mrs. Onesti?" the man replied; something about the way he said it made my eyes dart to my mother. He didn't look like a threatening person— he was on the short side, wearing khakis and a wrinkled button-down shirt. Maybe he had just heard how great our food was and wanted to compliment the chef. But then, why was my mother now gripping the counter so hard her knuckles turned white?

"Yes?" she said.

"Andrea Onesti? I'm here to serve you with a complaint. Can you sign here to accept service?"

I had no idea what the man was talking about. Everyone raved about our food, and our facilities were clean, so I couldn't think what someone would be complaining about. But when I glanced back at my mother, she seemed unsurprised.

"What is this in regards to?" she asked stiffly, but I could tell by the way she tilted her chin that she already knew.

"I'm just a process server, ma'am," the guy said. "But it looks like a complaint for foreclosure against you and"—he turned the paper in front of him around to read the name—"Dimitru Onesti?"

The way he butchered my father's name would

have been laughable if it weren't so obvious that something was very, very wrong. I'd heard the word *foreclosure* on the news a lot, and not in those human interest stories they like to show. The last program I'd seen had been about this neighborhood just outside of Austin that was almost completely deserted because the bank had had to take people's houses away.

My mother signed the paper the man presented to her, a bloom of red high on her cheekbones. He thanked her before he left, but she didn't reply. She stood at the counter, staring down at the stack of papers in front of her.

"Mama—" I began, but just then the phone rang. Could it be the bank?

My mother's voice was tight as she answered the phone. "It's for you," she said. "It's Christina."

"Hello?" It occurred to me that, even though I'd been to Christina's house several times, Christina had only been to the store on a handful of occasions, and she'd never been invited upstairs to see where we lived.

Maybe she'd never get to see the apartment now.

"What are you up to?" she asked, cutting to the chase with her usual forcefulness.

"Not much," I said automatically. Out of the corner of my eye, I could see my mother moving on to the onions I hadn't finished chopping for the traditional Romanian stew. "Uh, but I do need to get going."

I could hear the impatience in Christina's voice. "You need to get back to the nothing much that you're doing?" When Christina took that tone there was no stopping her. She probably *had* to tell me about a new leotard her mom had bought for her or something, and I would have to listen for five minutes before I could hang up. I loved Christina, but at times like this I wondered why it was always about her. Shouldn't a true friend have been able to sense my mood and ask how *I* was doing?

"What's up?" I asked finally.

"Okay," Christina said breathlessly, her annoyance replaced by excitement. "So, I told my mom about the dance, and she thought it was a great idea for us to go. I mean, you know how she is. She wants me to do extra sets of crunches at home to make sure I don't miss out on any training, but she loves the idea of us all getting dressed up and having a night out. She even offered to take us shopping for dresses and then out for coffee when we were finished. I'm going to invite Jessie and Britt, too, even though Britt doesn't need a dress. What do you say?"

"That sounds like . . . fun. But I really can't go. Sorry."

"Why not?" Christina demanded. "Ask your mom. Is she there? I want to hear you ask her. I bet she'd let you go."

Mama *would* probably have let me go. She was always saying I worked too hard with my homework and gymnastics, and that I should take some time to play, too. But it was almost impossible to think about fun when everything around me seemed like it was falling apart.

"She had to take the twins somewhere," I lied.

Christina's huffy sigh into the phone was so loud I held the receiver away from my ear. "All right, loser. Well, my mom and I are leaving for the mall in half an hour. If you change your mind, give me a call."

And then all I heard was a dial tone. I knew Christina didn't really mean it when she called me a loser—that was just the way she was. She'd probably called me that a million times, from the time I'd been too scared to jump off the high dive two summers ago to the time I'd said I didn't get the big deal with the latest teen heartthrob on the cover of one of her favorite magazines.

Still, it stung a little bit. Joking or not, that was probably how the other girls saw me, too. Good, dependable Noelle, who never gets in trouble and never does anything fun. What a loser.

"What did she want?" my mother asked. She'd efficiently chopped all of the onions and was now slicing up tomatoes. I knew that she wanted to have this stew simmering on the stove soon, so that it would have time to sit before lunchtime, the only really busy part of Sunday.

"Nothing." I motioned for the knife, intending to finish the vegetables, but my mother held it out of my reach.

"What did you say you couldn't go to?"

"Oh, just the mall," I said, making a face as though I hated the idea. "Christina, Jessie, and Britt are going shopping." I refrained from mentioning the dance.

My mother smiled, although it didn't quite reach her eyes. "That sounds like fun," she said. "Of course you should go!"

"You need me here."

"I can manage," she said, but she didn't look at me as she said it. Instead, she was already searching in her pockets, pulling out a crumpled five-dollar bill and a few singles. "I have eight dollars—that's enough to get some costume jewelry, right? You can bring something with you to eat, or else you can use your money to get something at the Food Court."

The necklace I'd admired at the mall before cost thirty dollars. There was no way I could ever spend that much money on something so frivolous.

"Christina's mom is going to take us out to lunch," I said, then realized I'd basically given in. I should've felt guiltier about it, but the truth was that I was happy to get away from this tense environment and spend the day with my friends. Then, of course, *that* made me feel guilty, so it was like I came full circle.

"Perfect!" she said, pressing the money into my hands. "Go call Christina. Her mom can pick you up, right?"

"Yeah." There was definitely no way I could ride my bike all the way to the mall and back, especially in the Texas summer heat. "Thanks, Mama."

"Have fun," she said, planting a wet kiss on my

forehead. Her hands still smelled like onions, which must've explained why my eyes watered a bit.

"Oh, my God, you *have* to try this one on." Christina thrust a strapless purple dress at me, and I automatically reached out to take it, less because I wanted it and more because I was afraid she'd stab me in the eye with the hanger if I didn't block her.

"It's not really my style," I said. And this was before I'd looked at the price tag: eighty dollars, which was *really* not my style. It was a good thing I thought that wearing anything strapless before you had any boobs was a huge mistake. I hung it back on the rack when Christina wasn't looking.

"I want to find something in green," Jessie was saying, sliding clothes from one side of the rack to the other as she scrutinized each one. "It's my favorite color."

"Plus, you can wear it on St. Patrick's Day and avoid getting pinched," Britt said. She was standing off to one side, smacking some gum that, knowing her, was four pieces of sugar-free watermelon flavor all mashed together. I almost envied her. She wasn't going to the dance, so no one expected her to buy anything.

Christina glared at Britt. "Green would look nice with your eyes," she said. "But you're not talking lime green, right? That would be totally bizarre."

Jessie flushed. "No, of course not," she said, but in a way that made me think maybe that had been her idea all along.

Christina surveyed the entire wall of dresses and wrinkled her nose. "I swear, all of these are meant for a fifth grade square dance or something. Let's go to the Taverna. You know they'll have a better selection there."

The selection would also be twice as expensive. I'd never been to the Taverna, but I'd heard about it from girls at my school. Once, this girl in my history class had been wearing a plain white T-shirt (short-sleeved, with a round neckline, nothing fancy) that she said had cost her fifty dollars at that store. The weird part was that she'd said it like it was something to be proud of. My mother bought me a pack of three of the same kind of shirt in the boys' underwear section at Walmart.

Jessie immediately agreed to move our shopping to another store, and Britt made a snarky comment about the *a* at the end of the Taverna's name but otherwise didn't object. There was no need for either of them to object—they'd probably been given sizable allowances to buy whatever they wanted. I even saw Mrs. Flores hand Christina her credit card before telling us to meet up with her at the coffee shop later.

The dresses at the Taverna *were* nicer, but a glance at their price tags confirmed my fears. Two hundred dollars for a minidress with spaghetti straps? You'd think there'd have been a price cut for all the material they'd skimped on. Christina saw me looking at the dress and must have misinterpreted my expression of disgust as something else, because she started rifling through the hangers looking for my size.

"You have the right idea," she said. "Shorter skirts make your legs look longer—good for us. But this pink is a little garish. Let's see if they have it in another color."

And that was how I found myself being pushed into the fitting rooms, clutching a deep blue, silky dress that would probably make me look like a little girl playing dress-up. I could hear the chattering of the other girls outside the dressing room as I slipped it over my head, leaving my jean shorts on underneath. I'd try it on, to humor Christina, but

I saw no reason to go all out when there was no way I'd buy it anyway.

Considering I had no curves to speak of, I fully expected the dress to hang in all the places it was supposed to cling, and for the waist to hit me somewhere halfway down my leg. But when I looked in the mirror, it was like I was a completely different person. The deep blue color made my skin luminous and my brown eyes huge, and my shoulders looked smooth and strong under the spaghetti straps, rather than bulky, which was what I'd feared. The dress was short, with a swirling skirt. I wriggled out of my jeans, and that made the dress fit a lot better on the bottom, but I would still have to wear a pair of my tighter gym shorts underneath or else be self-conscious all through the dance.

There was a pounding on the door, and I heard Jessie's voice. "Come on, Noelle," she called from the other side of the door. "We want to see."

I could've answered that the dress didn't fit, or that I didn't like it. But a stupid, vain part of me really wanted my friends to assure me that I actually looked . . . pretty.

When I opened the fitting-room door, there was no faking the looks on my friends' faces. I knew it looked great before they even said anything.

"Wow," Britt said. "What a dress."

I stood a little taller. "You think so?"

"Yeah," Jessie said. "You look amazing. You *have* to wear that to the dance."

My smile faltered as I remembered that I was about a hundred and ninety-two dollars away from being able to afford the dress. Not including tax.

"Most definitely," Christina agreed. "You're so lucky—you found the perfect dress right away. I've been looking all through the store, and I still can't decide."

I retreated back into the fitting room, only half listening to the conversation outside, as it went from Jessie's preference for an A-line skirt to Christina's opinions on what constituted too much bling for a middle-school dance. "If it was prom," I heard her say, "sure, I'd get something with sequins on the top *and* jeweled trim on the bottom. But that's totally tacky for this kind of dance, don't you think?"

Her words washed over me as I stared at my reflection in the mirror. If Scott could see me in this dress, maybe he wouldn't think I was such a kid. He might even think I was beautiful, something special. I had a vision of him escorting me to the dance, offering his arm as he smiled down at me with those perfect white teeth, his tie a dark blue to match my dress. He'd have called the night before to make sure he knew what color I was wearing, and also to find out if I preferred roses for my corsage or something else. *Surprise me*, I'd say breezily, and then he would give me an even better flower, one that he'd picked because it matched my eyes. . . .

I frowned at the reflection of my chocolate-colored eyes in the mirror. They might match a dried-up carnation, which would be a more likely possibility for a corsage. My daydream hadn't accounted for the fact that the dance was being held in the school gym and would be decorated with crepe paper, or the fact that I wasn't going to walk in there in this beautiful blue dress I couldn't afford. Or that there was no way Scott would ever escort me to a middle-school dance.

I heard a sharp rap at the door. "Are you finished?" Jessie asked. "Christina's trying on something now, and she wants all of our opinions."

I shimmied out of the dress, leaving it hanging in the fitting room. I mumbled something about wanting to look at other dresses before I made up my mind. It was a flimsy response, but before anyone could question me, I launched into enthusiastic feedback on the coral dress Christina had chosen. It was true that the color looked amazing with her smooth, tanned skin, so I felt only moderately guilty about gushing over it. Yes, I was trying to distract everyone from me, but I also sincerely meant the compliments.

Without the need for too much persuasion, Christina headed over to the front counter, happily extracted her mother's credit card from her purse, and charged the dress and a dangling crystal necklace to go with it. The bill came out to three hundred dollars, but she didn't even blink. I tried to think of all the things you could buy with that kind of money—my parents could have paid the electric bill, I could have gotten three custom-made leotards or a practice beam for my room, so I could work on my dance elements and basic acrobatic skills. Three hundred dollars was as much profit as my family's store pulled in some days. But when I closed my eyes, all I could see was a dress the color of the ocean.

We met up with Mrs. Flores at the coffee shop, although she sat at another table and played a game on her smartphone after Christina rolled her eyes when she tried to join us. I stirred my soy decaf slushee, which had sounded so good just a few minutes before but now seemed like a complete extravagance. The coffee slush was already melting a bit and settling toward the bottom of the cup.

Christina was still talking about her dress— saying that it wasn't what she had envisioned but that she thought that with the right accessories it could come pretty close—when Britt cut in. "You guys don't even know how lucky you are," she said. "I've never been to a school dance. Ever."

"They're really not all they're cracked up to be," Jessie said. "It's not like in the movies, where some awesome band plays and the boy you like finally confesses his feelings. You dress up, and then you wish that you were at home in sweatpants watching TV instead. Or at least, that's how the Valentine's Day dance was last year."

I hadn't gone to the Valentine's Day dance, and this year they had canceled it because of some inappropriate behavior on the part of the eighth grade boys. I'd never found out exactly what had happened, but it had had something to do with the assistant principal's golf cart.

"Still," Britt said. "It'd be nice to have something like that to look forward to. What am I going to do, dance around the living room with my grandmother?"

There were days when I wished I was homeschooled. It seemed like it would be so much easier—not having to worry about other kids' comments, where to sit at lunch, whether your teacher liked you or whether she thought you used gymnastics as an excuse to get out of work. I was so paranoid about that last one that I made it a point never to turn in an assignment late, even when I had a huge competition and it meant that I had to spend all of my free time typing up a report about the Battle of the Alamo when all I really wanted to do was nap.

"I told you that we could get you in," Christina said. "It's not like there's a velvet rope at these things."

Britt shrugged with one shoulder.

Jessie idly tapped a finger on the cup of her lemonade–iced tea. "It's probably for the best that all I have to worry about this summer is qualifying for Elite," she said.

It was a random thing to say, but we waited her out to see where she was going to go with it.

Of the four of us, Jessie was the only one who was not eligible for Elite-level competition, which meant that there was no way she'd be competing at Junior Nationals with the rest of us—assuming that Christina and Britt made the cut at the U.S. Classic, and assuming that I could scrounge up the nerve to ask my parents about going.

"That's not *all* you have to worry about," Christina pointed out. I caught Britt's wide-eyed look as we both thought the same thing. I really hoped this wasn't Christina's insensitive way of referring to Jessie's eating disorder. Because she could be thoughtless sometimes, but that would just have been too much.

But Christina continued without skipping a beat. "I mean, you've got to worry about whether you'll find a hot guy to dance with on Friday."

I let out a nervous laugh that sounded more like a yelp. "Yeah, right," I said, hoping that no one had caught that weird little sound. "Like there's a boy in the entire school who could be classified as 'hot.'"

One corner of Christina's mouth lifted in acknowledgment of this sad truth. "There are some moderately cute ones, though," she said. "Like Justin . . . even though he's going out with that ditz Tessa. Or Zac, if you ignore his narcissistic personality. Or . . ."

"David Schaeffer," Jessie whispered.

Christina wrinkled her nose. "He's okay," she said. "But he's always got his face jammed in a book. Don't get me wrong, reading is awesome and blah-blah-blah, like Mrs. Bishop is always going on about, but he walked right into me the other day. I was at my locker and he could've knocked me over. He didn't even look up."

"No, I mean David Schaeffer is *coming over here*," Jessie said.

Christina looked stricken for just a moment, as though she was afraid he might've overheard her, but then she pasted a smile on her face. "David, hey!" she said as he approached our table.

David had been in some of my classes since sixth grade, and this year he was in my English class and my P.E. period. Since I sat in the very front row in English, I was barely aware of his sitting two rows back. And I had P.E. every morning, but got to skip it for gymnastics practice and have that count toward my physical education requirement. Luckily, the school recognized that when you could press into a one-armed handstand and support that position for ten seconds, it seemed kind of redundant to make you walk laps around the track to get a stupid stamp on your hand.

In fact, the only time I'd ever really talked to David was the one day I'd been forced to go to P.E. Morning practice had been unexpectedly cut short because of a power outage at the gym, and so I'd ridden my bike to school just in time for the second half of P.E. All of the other kids were in the middle of a baseball game, and the coach was so surprised to see me that she let me sit on the bleachers to watch. David had been sitting there, too, reading a book, as usual.

I'd caught a glimpse of the front cover and seen that he was reading the seventh book in the Harry Potter series. It was one of my favorites, and I'd read each of the books at least eight times. I considered asking him what he thought about the books versus the movies, but starting conversations has never been my strong suit. So instead I just sat there until he glanced up.

"I forgot my uniform," he said. It was one of those stupid rules that made me glad I got to skip P.E.: if you didn't have the ugly orange T-shirt with your name written on it in black Sharpie and the ugly navy shorts that hit you at the most awkward part of the thigh, then you weren't allowed to participate. And if you missed too many days, you could fail P.E., which would have been completely lame.

But David didn't seem to care, because a few minutes later he confessed, "Actually, my uniform is in my locker. I just didn't bother to put it on, because I'm on the second-to-last chapter and I'd rather finish this book than wait thirty minutes for my turn to run around the bases."

Using that as a conversation starter, I finally got up the nerve to ask him about Harry Potter, and we ended up spending the next twenty minutes discussing how we liked Daniel Radcliffe in the early movies but found him a little annoying later on, and how we hated people who spoiled major plot points before you had a chance to read the books yourself.

Even though I hadn't really talked to David since then, it still felt natural to smile and wave at him when I saw him now. He grinned back, and for the first time, I noticed that he had a very nice smile. He had a way of making you feel like he was thrilled to see you, even when you weren't close friends.

"Hi, Noelle," he said. "Christina, Jessie. And . . ." He looked inquiringly at Britt, who extended her hand and introduced herself.

"Where's your book?" Christina asked, and inwardly I cringed a little. She could be so abrasive sometimes. But David didn't seem to take offense.

"I'm in between right now," he said with a laugh. "Any suggestions?"

"You mean, to read for *pleasure*? Hardly." Christina wasn't exactly the biggest reader in the world. Not that she did poorly in school—she got decent grades. You had to, if you wanted to stay on the Elite team at Texas Twisters. It was one of Mo's rules. But Christina didn't believe in reading a book when you could get the story from a movie or on TV.

"What about you?" he asked, turning to me.

I knew that David would pick up just about any book, but I also knew from observation that he seemed to like fantasy series. I named a few off the top of my head, and he appeared to take each suggestion seriously, mulling it over and asking questions about why I would recommend it.

"So, you've read all of those?" he asked.

I flushed a little. "Well, no," I said. "Not all. It's

hard to find the time. Summer is when all the big competitions are, so I'm training a lot."

I wondered if I shouldn't have mentioned gymnastics. Obviously, David knew that I was a serious athlete—the whole school knew, thanks to an embarrassing congratulatory announcement they'd made on the morning show after I won the gold on beam in last year's state championships. But it seemed to me like people always got awkward when it came up, as though it was a reminder of how little I resembled a real human being.

"That's cool," David said, and he didn't seem weirded out, although he could just have been hiding it well. "Are you too busy to go to the dance on Friday?"

"We're definitely going," Christina broke in, glancing at me with this strange, shiny-eyed look, then turning back to David. "What about you?"

"I was thinking about it," he said, still looking at me. "I'm not really good at dancing."

"What's there to it?" Britt said. "You just hold on to someone and sway back and forth. And for the fast stuff, you just let go of the person and move faster. It's a no-brainer."

It looked as though Christina nudged Jessie,

but I couldn't think why. Jessie's elbows *were* encroaching a bit on Christina's side of the table, so maybe that was it. "Plus," Christina added, "Jessie or I would be happy to hold your book for you if you wanted to take a spin on the dance floor. Right, Jessie?"

"Of course," Jessie said brightly.

David laughed. "Okay, thanks. I'll keep that in mind. I've got to get going, though. My mom's waiting for me. I'll see you guys around?"

"Definitely," Jessie and Christina said in unison.

"See you, Noelle," he said, touching my shoulder briefly. It was a grazing touch, but it was so unexpected that it caught me off guard. It felt weird—not bad, just . . . interesting.

"'Bye," I said.

Christina craned her neck until she saw David disappear around the corner, and then she turned to me. "Oh. My. God."

"What?"

She shook her head. "You can't be serious," she said.

I was totally lost now. "Why?" I asked, glancing at Jessie and Britt. It was Britt who finally answered.

"That guy *likes* you," she said. "Duh."

"No, he doesn't," I protested automatically. "He can't."

"Like, it's against the law?" Britt ticked off her points on her fingers. "He clearly was asking if *you* were going to the dance, and he asked *you* about books you'd read."

"So? We're friends." It made sense to me. If I ran into David and his friends at the mall, of course I'd talk mostly to David, since he'd be the one I knew the best. It didn't mean anything.

"For now," Jessie said. "But wait until the dance."

I still didn't know if I was even going to go to the dance, but I knew better than to open that can of worms. I tried to replay in my head the conversation we'd just had with David, searching for any clue that the other girls were right, but I couldn't imagine that they were. The very idea made me want to run as far as I could away from the dance on Friday.

I mean, I didn't like David—I couldn't. When I gazed into Scott's bright blue eyes, my heart beat as quickly as if I'd just completed back-to-back tumbling passes. When I looked into David's eyes behind his glasses (they were an unusual amber brown color, I'd noticed today), my heart beat at the same pace it would have if I'd been watching one of my teammates flip across the floor. And while I could barely get a word out without stuttering when I talked to Scott, I found talking to David surprisingly easy. Even that day in the bleachers, twenty minutes had flown by as we moved from subject to subject.

Mrs. Flores signaled to us that it was time to go, and we gathered up our trash. I realized I'd barely touched my drink. It was only later, watching the shadowy patterns of the trees through the window as Mrs. Flores drove me home, that it dawned on me that I also hadn't thought about Junior Nationals much since arriving at the mall. My mind had been too much on the dance and the dress and David. I reminded myself that I couldn't afford to lose focus, but then I remembered—I might not have anything to focus on, if I wasn't going to go to Junior Nationals in the first place. If that was the case, then I could obsess about anything I wanted to.

That idea wasn't as comforting as I'd once thought it would be.

Six

I spent the next few days awkwardly avoiding David in English, and dodging Mo after practice in case she asked me about the parents' meeting. When there were only three sets of parents invited, I guess it was pretty obvious if you didn't get an RSVP from one of them.

Although I usually felt proud of the level of trust Mo had in me, this time I only felt guilty. She could've called my house directly, instead of asking me whether my parents were planning to attend. But I was sure she couldn't have conceived of a scenario where I hid the information packet in the drawer of my bedside table, and only took it out late at night when everyone else was asleep. She couldn't have imagined how many times I'd closed my eyes and tried to envision myself boarding a plane to Philadelphia and sharing a hotel room with Christina and Britt, every nerve end in my body buzzing with anticipation of the biggest competition of my life. She couldn't have fathomed how many times I'd imagined winning the all-around gold—or sometimes, in my grandest dreams, sweeping every single event.

To Mo, it was a cut-and-dried decision. I had a chance to go to a competition that could define the rest of my career, so of course I would do everything in my power to go. Of course I would ask my parents and let them figure out how to make my dream come true, probably in the same way they'd managed to eke out the payments for my training every month.

And maybe it should've been that simple. But at this point, every day that passed where my parents didn't know about the upcoming competition was another day during which we lost the opportunity to try to earn the money for me to go. I felt the delay like a tightening vise, but I still found myself responding to my parents' questions about gym with monosyllabic answers.

"So, your parents come tomorrow?" Mo asked at the end of Thursday's practice. "I don't hear from them."

"They can't." It was amazing how quickly the lie fell off my tongue. "There's a big event at the store, and they can't get away."

Mo's eyes were an inky black—not dark brown, but black—and they were completely unreadable as she looked at me. I thought for sure she could see right through me, and I opened my mouth, ready to add to my story, when she shook her head.

"They read packet, yes?" she asked. "Make sure they know to register for hotel early. Athletes have rooms reserved, but other rooms fill up quick."

I hadn't even thought about the fact that they would have to pay not only half the cost of the room I would share with a teammate, but also for another room, for the family. "Okay, thanks," I said, not wanting to compound my lie any further.

I tried to make my escape, but Mo touched my arm. "Noelle," she said. "I know you worry. You do not need to."

Did she suspect something? I'd never been a good liar. My mother always said that even when I was little, she had known immediately when I'd snuck a treat. If she asked me directly about it, I'd shake my head, but my hands would go immediately to my bottom, as though I was anticipating a spanking. My mother said she rarely needed to actually punish me—my fear of punishment was enough.

So it was possible that, though I thought I was cooking up a totally believable story, my face gave me away. Mo had her fingers in every aspect of this gym's operation, including admissions and billing, as well as coaching and recruitment.

Or maybe Mo knew about our plans to go to the dance, and disapproved. It was happening tomorrow, after all.

"You are making good progress," Mo said, and for a second I couldn't figure out what she was referring to. Progress on telling my parents about Nationals? Because I wasn't making any progress on that front at all. I'd had multiple opportunities to bring it up—I'd even tried to steer conversations in that direction, but I always chickened out at the last minute. Progress on the dance? Because I still didn't have my dress, even though Christina had offered multiple times to buy the blue one for me if I really wanted it.

Mo must've seen the confusion on my face,

because she clarified her meaning. "On your dismount," she said. "You are making good progress. I know you will have it by Nationals, and you have very good chance at winning medal."

Mo was not exactly the kind of person I imagined playing the lottery, so I knew if she said she thought I could win a medal, she wasn't just taking a gamble. It made me feel proud and confident. And it made me feel suddenly angry that I might not get my opportunity, when there were other gymnasts who weren't as good but who weren't held back by financial problems. It also made me feel guiltier than I'd ever thought possible.

"Thanks," I said, hoping my smile didn't show any of these emotions. I thought about how appalled I'd been only a week earlier, when Christina had suggested not telling Mo about the dance, in case she objected to our going. And now I was not only withholding information—I was actively lying. I was doing it to avoid conflict, but I knew that the eventual fallout would be way worse. Still, that didn't stop me from feeling relieved that I could bury my head in the sand for at least another day, and pretend everything was fine.

* * *

If my life were one of those feel-good ABC Family shows, I would've found a way to earn the money for that perfect dress I'd tried on in the Taverna. Or maybe I'd have a quirky friend who would sew me a copy of the dress; it wouldn't be the same, but somehow it would be even better, because she'd made it with love.

Although my script could have included Christina's buying the dress for me, that seemed uncomfortably close to a miniseries called *Noelle Onesti: Charity Case*, so I shrugged her off whenever she offered.

Instead, I found myself getting ready for the dance by changing into the same black dress I'd worn to Papu's funeral the year before. Rather than spaghetti straps, it had cap sleeves and a rounded collar. And instead of a flirty skirt that twirled around my legs, it had a straight, knee-length skirt that was more appropriate for a secretary than a girl at a school dance.

I had a couple of other dresses, including a flowered one I'd worn to the Easter service at St. Mary Magdalene, but these seemed so babyish when I tried them on. The black dress might have been dull, but at least it made me feel somewhat sophisticated.

Both Christina's and Britt's parents were at the meeting at the gym, so Jessie's mother was driving us all to the dance. I'd told my parents about the dance but still hadn't mentioned the meeting, so I said a quick good-bye on my way out the door and hoped they wouldn't come out to talk to Jessie's mom. It would have been too easy for her to ask them why they hadn't been at the meeting, and then the entire story would blow up in my face.

Christina couldn't hide her look of horror when I climbed into the backseat with her. "*That's* what you're wearing?" she asked. "It looks like you're going to a funeral."

Which had been the original purpose of the dress, of course, but I didn't say that. "It seemed stupid to make such a big deal about a middle-school dance. As you said, it's not like it's prom."

Christina self-consciously patted her hair, which was coiled in an intricate updo that I knew she'd probably gone to a salon to get.

"*You* look beautiful," I said, because she did. I didn't want her to think I was making a pointed dig about her trying too hard, when really I just wanted to get the focus off my boring dress.

I had put on a little mascara and some lip gloss

for the occasion, which made me feel very grown-up (I'd tried on some of Christina's eye shadow before, but didn't like the crusty way it felt on my eyelids with all that glitter). I usually wore makeup only for big competitions, but that was different. Those cosmetics were designed to stay on my face for hours while I sweated and blew chalk everywhere, and were also made to be seen by the judges and up in the stands. They really bore more resemblance to Halloween makeup than to anything else.

I didn't see Jessie's dress until we all got out of the car, since she had been sitting up front. It was the color of the grass on a golf course, which I knew was exactly what she'd wanted. The fabric had a slight sheen to it and caught the light as we walked up to the door of the gym, where teachers were checking student IDs.

"See, I don't think Britt could've come after all," Jessie said.

Christina waved her hand. "There's always a way. What do they care if some extra kids are sipping off the watered-down punch?"

As much as I'd resisted coming to the dance, if it hadn't even been an option for me to go I would've felt bummed out. I made a mental note to be extra nice to Britt when we were back in the gym tomorrow, to try to make up for the fact that she was probably sitting at home tonight watching a marathon of *America's Next Top Model* while we had fun at the dance. Although right now, with the butterflies fluttering in my stomach, *Top Model* kind of seemed like more fun.

I tried to picture Scott in this environment, but I couldn't. As I'd expected, the decorations consisted of orange and blue crepe paper hanging from the ceiling and a couple of hand-markered banners wishing all the eighth graders good luck. Scott might not have been much taller than many of the boys—according to his USA Gymnastics profile online (as part of the Junior National men's team), he was five foot six—but he had more muscle and more maturity. He probably wouldn't have pulled any pranks with a golf cart or thrown wet toilet paper at the ceilings of the bathrooms until the school took all of the toilet paper out and made us carry rolls from our classroom stash as our "hall passes." There were boys on the dance floor doing the robot or awkwardly jabbing their arms in the air in time to the hip-hop beat; I imagined what Scott would look like dancing.

It was difficult to see anyone *not* dancing like an idiot to this kind of music, so instead I tried to picture him swaying slowly to a John Mayer song. But for some reason, I could only see him as if from a distance, looking down into some girl's eyes, though I could never imagine myself as that girl, in that moment. I squeezed my eyes shut to concentrate.

"I'm already bored," Jessie said.

Christina toyed with the beaded strap of her tiny purse. "We just got here. Chill out."

"Noelle's fallen asleep."

I opened my eyes. "I'm not asleep," I protested. I *had* been daydreaming, but I wasn't about to bring that up.

Christina suggested that we get some punch, as something to do, and so, minutes later, we were back, standing in the same corner, only this time with fruit punch that was so diluted it was more pink than red. It didn't take long before we were discussing gymnastics. The gym pro shop sold T-shirts that said things like GYMNASTICS IS LIFE— THE REST IS JUST DETAILS, and it was pretty much true. When you spent more of your life in the gym than anywhere else, it was hard to find other things to talk about.

"I'm going away for a week," Jessie said. "But it shouldn't interfere too much with training, since I'll be gone while you guys are at Nationals. Mo and Cheng won't even be here, anyway, so you know I'd just be doing repetitive stuff with one of the assistant coaches."

Even a week away from practice was a lot, though. It was like cramming for an exam and then having spring break before you actually took the test. You could never expect to remember everything that you knew before the vacation. A week away from practice meant that your muscle memory might've had the chance to atrophy in much the same way.

I didn't want to ask Jessie why she was taking a week off, since the last time she'd done that had been when she began treatment for her eating disorder just last month. But she provided the answer without being prompted, saying, "I get to stay with my dad. He's going to take me camping and everything."

Jessie's parents were divorced, and she lived with her mom and her stepdad. In all of the years I'd known Jessie, I'd never met her father, and I'd only heard about him a few times. I knew that he was an anchor on a television station that broadcast out of Houston, and that Jessie recorded his segments. I also knew that she was supposed to spend some Christmases and occasional weekends with him, but that it never worked out.

But if she was talking about it this time, that must have meant there was a more definite plan. "That's cool," I said. "My dad used to take us camping; we'd make s'mores and try to find constellations, even though we always ended up making up new ones."

I realized that it had been years since we'd last been camping, or on any vacation, for that matter. The last time had been when I was eight, and we'd gone to Galveston Island for a weekend. Of course, then I'd just been a Level Seven gymnast, competing at meets held at rival gyms, with chairs set up for the parents to sit in and watch. That was back in the days when they'd given a ribbon to every single girl who participated, even if it meant you got the pink ribbon for coming in in eleventh place in the Level Seven, age 8–10 category.

It was yet another sacrifice my family had made for my gymnastics. With the money that Junior Nationals would cost them, my parents could have afforded to fly my older brothers to Romania stay with relatives, or take the whole family to Florida or something. It hardly seemed fair.

"It's going to be awesome," Jessie said, snapping me back into the present. "And it'll be just me and my dad—the stepmonster's not even going to come."

I'd heard a little bit more about Jessie's stepmother than I had about her father, which had never struck me as odd until now. I knew that she didn't work, and that she spent her time on ridiculous things like spreading all her hats on the bed to organize them. "Who has that many hats?" Jessie had said. "And who needs to organize them that often?"

"I can't afford to miss much practice," Christina said. "I know I'm already behind, since I just qualified for Elite. Britt's been Elite for a while, and Noelle's earned her place at Nationals. And now my mother wants me to meet with a publicity coach, so that's one more thing to worry about."

Jessie and I exchanged a look, and Christina caught it and rushed to explain. "I know I haven't won anything yet," she said, tripping over her words a little. "But I guess once my mother saw Scott's interview, she got it into her head that I should start practicing being comfortable in front of the media."

I remembered how upset Christina had been that the news crew wasn't there to interview her, and I wondered if she'd had more to do with the hiring of this publicity coach than she was letting on. It was the kind of thing that Mrs. Flores would totally have done, but it was also the kind of thing that Christina would eat up.

It was good that Christina hadn't mentioned this in front of Britt, because Britt would've laughed in her face. Christina was the most intimidating person I knew in some ways, but Britt was the most fearless. She'd make some crack about how stupid it was to pay someone five thousand dollars to basically tell you to smile a lot and appear humble. Then again, if there was anyone who needed that kind of lesson, it was probably Britt or Christina.

Christina turned to me. "You should think about doing the same thing," she said. "Let's be honest; you have the best chance of any of us of winning a medal."

I laughed, trying to turn it into a joke. "I hope not," I said. "I want to win, of course, but do you know how many Junior National champions went on to win Olympic gold? Let's just say I'd rather peak later in my career."

It was something I told myself, to help prepare for the disappointment of losing a competition. I always reminded myself that the Olympics were the ultimate goal, and no one cared how many medals you'd won at the Junior level if you couldn't make your mark at the Olympics. Deep down, of course, I wanted it all. I wanted to sweep the gold medals at every competition I went to, and then continue on to be the greatest Olympic champion that the world had ever known.

But I was starting to realize that champions were, at least to some extent, bought rather than made. The girls who could afford to travel to the Pan American Games or who could afford private choreographers and specialist coaches to perfect individual routines were always going to have an edge over girls like me, who were already financially maxed out. I was lucky to train at what was probably the best gymnastics facility in the southwest, and one of the top five in the country.

As excessive as I thought a publicity coach sounded, it must be nice to have the option. And yet it was the kind of thing that Christina took for granted, like the custom leotards she got every year for Christmas or the mini training area her parents had built for her in their basement. I hated myself for the uncharitable thought, considering that Christina had been more than willing to help me out with money on many occasions, but there it was.

Just then, a slow song came on, and the dance floor cleared except for the couples, who started to gently sway to the music. It was surprising how uncomfortable some people looked as they shuffled from side to side. I tried not to let it affect my perfect vision of dancing with Scott, but it interfered anyway. Now I could only picture us from a distance, taking hesitant steps that barely masqueraded as rhythm.

"This is kind of lame," Jessie said. "I know the boys in our school are savages, but you'd think at least one of them would've asked us to dance by now."

"Speaking of . . ." Christina muttered. Jessie and I turned to see David Schaeffer heading toward us.

I hadn't expected him to clean up so well. He was wearing a blazer over his usual black T-shirt and jeans, and his hair was gelled into spikes. I also noticed he was short, for a guy, but kind of a perfect height for me, since I was so short myself. When he saw me, he smiled, and I nervously looked away.

"Enjoying yourselves?" he asked as he joined our group.

"I was saying how boring this is so far," Jessie said. "I mean, if we wanted to stand around and talk about gymnastics, we could hang out after practice."

"But then you wouldn't have this delicious punch," David said wryly, holding up his glass in a mock salute.

Christina and Jessie giggled, but I could barely manage a smile. I felt all wound up for some reason, like I was a coil stretched to its breaking point. I told myself it was because it was so hot inside the gym, and I tried to take some deep breaths. I was focusing so much on the act of inhaling and exhaling that it took me a few seconds to register that David was talking to me.

"Sorry?" I said.

He flushed, and I wondered if he also thought it was too warm. "If you don't want to, that's cool," he said. "I just thought that this song wasn't as heinously awful as the rest of the music they've been playing."

Now I was more confused than before. I tried to listen to what song was playing, but it was like the notes were all out of order—I couldn't even process the melody. "What?"

Christina gave me a shove. "She'd love to dance with you," she said.

Now it was my turn to blush as I let David lead me to the dance floor, his hand letting go of mine only when he rested both palms on my waist and I instinctively wrapped my arms around his neck. I tried to imagine what we must look like to my friends, and whether they were laughing at us as we became yet another cringeworthy couple performing a mime of a slow dance. But for some reason it was almost like I had the opposite problem from the one I'd had with my daydream about Scott: I couldn't remove myself from the situation enough to picture us as an outsider might. I could only look up at David and glance away when his eyes met mine.

"So . . ." I searched for something to say. "Read any good books lately?"

He listed a couple of titles, but I wasn't listening. I was thinking about how, even though David was nice and smelled really good, I couldn't help comparing him to Scott. And while I did like David, Scott was so perfect that it was hard for anyone to measure up, even someone as fun to talk to as David.

I had just reached the conclusion that I definitely did *not* like David as more than just a friend when it hit me that he might feel differently. I'd denied it to my friends at the mall, but it became kind of obvious when his face started to come closer. I turned my cheek just in time, and his lips only brushed the corner of mine.

"What are you doing?" I squeaked.

His face was as pink as the lukewarm punch they were serving. "Kissing you?" he said, his voice rising on the last syllable in what was more a question than a statement.

"You could've warned me first!" If he had said something to indicate that he was about to kiss me, I would've stopped it. Right?

We had stopped swaying and were now just standing in the corner of the dance floor, his hands still at my waist. I wanted to glance behind me and see if my friends were watching, but I knew they must be, and I felt even more mortified.

"I don't know. In movies and stuff they always just, you know, *kiss*. I thought it would be more romantic than telling you that I liked you."

"But we were talking about books we'd read," I said. "What's romantic about that?"

If possible, David only got more flustered. "I wasn't thinking about it," he said. "I didn't even know we were talking about books. I mean, of course I *knew*, because you asked me about what I'd read and I was telling you about why I hated it when they turned good books into movies because they always messed up absolutely key details, but I was also thinking about how to tell you that I liked you, and I thought . . . I guess I thought kissing you was a good idea."

Suddenly, all I could focus on was the fact that David Schaeffer had *kissed* me. My first kiss. The first kiss that I'd been saving for Scott, who was supposed to give it to me in the park, after he'd pushed me on a swing, or at a romantic picnic, or even under the mistletoe at the Texas Twisters Christmas party. It wasn't supposed to be an awkward brush of the lips at a middle-school dance, wearing the wrong dress and being kissed by the wrong guy.

"I have to go," I said.

And then I was running off the dance floor, past Jessie and Christina, who were both staring after me with their mouths open. This was why things would have been much easier if I just went to school, gym, and home. I knew how to handle a problem like not getting enough rotation on an Arabian double front, but put me in a situation like this . . . and I was just hopeless.

Seven

The last time Mihai had come into my room, I was nine years old and had convinced him to play Barbies with me. At a yard sale, Mama had bought me a special Barbie doll that had flexible joints, and I used to play with her for hours, pretending that she was a gymnast competing at the biggest meet of her life. I made up whole routines consisting of my favorite moves from all of my gymnastics idols' routines and crafted medals out of bits of tinfoil and ribbon. Mihai would make fun of me, but he could usually be persuaded to play one of the judges or a rival gymnast if I let him take some liberties with my story line. This usually consisted of the judge's doubling as a BMX star, or the rival gymnast's being the first ever to execute a quadruple-twisting, quadruple-flipping vault.

So when Mihai showed up now, I was a little surprised. It had been a few days since the dance, and even though I'd had some time to calm down and reflect on the whole weird situation with David Schaeffer, I was still spending most of my time outside of the gym shut up in my bedroom, staring at the ceiling.

"What's up?" he asked, leaning against the doorframe.

It had to be obvious that *nothing* was, but I sat up in bed to face him. "Just thinking," I said.

"As exciting as that sounds," Mihai said, "why don't you come on a walk with me, instead?"

We told Radu where we were going on our way out. He didn't look happy to be the only one of us working in the store, but I was too intrigued by this rare opportunity to hang out with Mihai to really care. Was he going to ask me to cover for him while he escaped for the night? It was hard for me to imagine refusing my favorite brother (nothing against Radu or the twins, but the twins pulled my hair and screamed too much, and Radu liked to tease me), but I couldn't imagine going against my parents, either.

There were some trees and overgrown bushes behind the store, and Mihai led me to the chain-link gate at the end of the street, which kept trespassers from entering.

"It's locked," I pointed out.

He raised his eyebrow. "So? I thought you were a vault champion."

He set one fake-Converse-clad foot in one of the diamond-shaped spaces and swung his other leg over in a fluid motion. Then he wiped his hands on his jeans and gave me a daring grin. "Well?"

When signs said things like NO TRESPASSING in huge red letters, I tended to take them pretty seriously. But it was not like I'd ever seen cops out there in the entire time we'd lived above the store, and nobody was using this land for anything. I just hoped nobody cared if they saw two kids walking around there. Unless Mihai had some other mischief planned besides just hanging out, which, knowing him, was totally possible.

I hesitated for another second before following him up and over the fence. Maybe it was because I was nervous, but my movements weren't nearly as agile as his, and he had to help me over. I let out a shaky breath once my feet hit the ground.

"I consider myself more of a beam champion," I said.

"Come on," he said, taking my hand. "I want to show you something."

We stepped over some tree roots and dead leaves as we wound our way deeper into the woods, until eventually we came to a clearing. The sun shone through the trees as if in a painting, as if there was a heavenly spotlight on this secret hideaway. It was beautiful, but I couldn't figure out what it was that Mihai wanted me to see.

"Is this it?" I asked.

"*Shhh,*" he said.

"What *is* it?" I asked.

"*Shhh.*"

When I was younger, Mihai used to love to play this game on car trips where he would exclaim over something outside the window. I would press my nose to the glass or turn completely around in my seat, trying to see what it was that he had seen, and finally I'd ask him about it. It always turned out to be nothing, every time. And yet I fell for it again and again, thinking that Mihai had spotted something amazing through the window that I wouldn't have wanted to miss out on.

I wondered if he remembered that game as well as I did, and if that was the game he was playing right now.

"Tell me what I should be looking at," I said.

Mihai squeezed my hand before letting it go.

"Breathe, Noelle."

And so I did. I closed my eyes and felt my chest rise and fall as I inhaled the smell of birch trees and exhaled deep, even breaths. For those endless moments, I let go of some of the stresses in my life. It was easy to pretend that everything was going to be okay while standing in the middle of this clearing, feeling the shade of the trees at my back and the warmth of the setting sun on my face.

"Better?" Mihai asked, his eyes on me.

I nodded. I didn't need to ask now what he'd wanted me to see. "How did you know?" I asked.

"Are you kidding? You've been a stress-ball for the past two weeks. I may not be around much, but I'm not blind."

"Mama and Tata seem to be," I said without thinking, then wondered where that had come from. This whole time, I'd been totally focused on hiding things from them, but was that just a cover? Did I really want them to force the issue, by letting them see that I was distracted?

"I come here to think," Mihai said, "when I just need to get away from everything. I thought you might be able to use a little of that relaxation."

"Is this where you disappear to?" I asked hesitantly. I didn't want to ruin the tentative truce Mihai and I had reached in this magical place that seemed so removed from the rest of the world, but I also really wanted to know.

"Sometimes," he said vaguely. "Listen, I'm sorry about the other night. I didn't mean what I said, about you having no life."

I shrugged. It was kind of true. And mostly, I really didn't mind. I was happy to spend eight hours a day at the gym. I loved the feeling of mastering a difficult skill that I'd been working on for a while. I loved the smell of foam mats and chalk and sweat. I loved the sound of the springs in the beam as I landed a jump. I might not have had much of a life outside the gym, but when gymnastics meant everything, who needed anything else?

And then, before I could stop myself, the whole sorry saga started pouring out. I told Mihai about the guy who had come to the store tossing around words like *foreclosure*; about Junior Nationals and how much they would cost; and then I threw humility to the wind and revealed how confident I was that I could come away with at least one medal, if only I could go in the first place. I left out the whole part about Scott and David, because who wants to discuss boys with their *brother*, but otherwise I let the words trip over each other and fill the silence of the clearing while Mihai listened.

When he was finally able to get a comment in, it was one I'd expected but hoped not to hear. "You have to tell Mama and Tata," he said. "You know that, right?"

"I can't," I said. "I know we don't have the money."

"How much are we talking?"

I did some mental calculations as to the cost of the hotel, the flight, and the custom red leotard that Mo had been reminding me about all week, and named an amount that made Mihai whistle. Of course, I'd known it was an impossible sum, but his reaction still made my heart fall into my stomach.

"So, what do you see as your options?" he asked. "Because missing Nationals isn't exactly one of them."

The thought of staying home while Christina and Britt went on to compete made me want to throw up. And I felt that helpless anger rise up in my throat, the familiar burn that kept coming back no matter how I tried to ignore it. Out of the whole Elite team at Texas Twisters, *I* was the only one who'd already qualified for Nationals. I'd shown Coach Piserchia everything I had back in training camp, and he'd chosen me as one of only three gymnasts who were good enough to skip the U.S. Classic and go right to Nationals. Britt and Christina hadn't even qualified yet, and their parents were already attending meetings and booking hotel rooms and making plans to go to Philadelphia. It didn't seem fair.

I knew Mihai was right. Missing out on the biggest competition of my life so far was *not* an option. But it was impossible for me to consider the alternative. It wasn't like my parents had that kind of money in savings—if they had, I'm sure we wouldn't have had a leak in our roof, or been in danger of the bank's taking the house and store. I couldn't ask them to shell out all that money for what was essentially one weekend for me, when we'd had to put pots out every time it rained for over a year. We could lose everything.

"Promise me you won't tell them," I said.

His brown eyes held mine. "Promise me that you will."

"Mihai." My voice was low and insistent. "*Promise.*"

He gave me the Boy Scout's salute, even though he'd never been a Boy Scout. "Okay, I promise," he said. "But you really have to tell them, Noelle. Soon. The longer you wait, it's only going to make it harder for them to come up with that money."

"I know."

We stood there for a few moments, watching a sparrow that hopped from one tree branch to another in the fading light. It was getting to be dusk, and I knew that Tata would have retreated into the storeroom just in time for the after-work crowd. We couldn't leave Radu to handle the rush alone.

Mihai was obviously thinking the same thing, because he started back the way we had come. As he helped me over the fence one more time, I thought how nice it was to have my brother back. I also thought about the promise he'd made me, and wondered if he realized that I had never made any in return.

* * *

A week had passed since the dance, and Christina and I were stretching on the floor, waiting for Jessie and Britt to emerge from the bathroom and join us. Christina kept looking at me weirdly, and after I'd already run a self-conscious tongue over my teeth, worried I might have had something stuck there, I finally asked her what was up.

"Why didn't you let me buy you that blue dress?" she asked.

It took me so by surprise that I stuttered as I tried to respond. "I told you," I said, "I was still looking around."

"And you decided that the ugly black thing you wore was *better*?" That was Christina—always blunt.

"Look, not everyone has hundreds of dollars to spend for one stupid outfit," I snapped.

Christina's eyes turned blacker than usual, and for a second I thought she was going to strike back. Christina is not exactly known for keeping her temper. But instead, her voice went soft. "Look, Noelle—" She stopped, as though unsure how to phrase it. "I mean, I know that your family doesn't have as much money as mine. And my mom likes shopping. She likes to buy things. You've come over to my house so much you're like a second daughter, only you're not as bratty as I am. So it's really not a big deal if you need help . . . with anything."

It was a struggle for me to match her quiet tone, when all I wanted to do was scream. "Maybe we all don't live in mansions," I whispered hotly, "but that doesn't mean that we're charity cases, either."

Christina shook her head. "Sorry, that came out wrong. I'm just saying, I know you haven't gotten your custom leo yet. And I know my mom wouldn't mind—"

Luckily, I was spared the rest of this humiliating discussion when Jessie and Britt plopped themselves down on the floor next to us. "What are you guys talking about?" Britt asked.

"Nothing," I said, while Christina, at the same time replied, "The dance."

Jessie's face brightened in a way I shouldn't have trusted. "I know you don't want to talk about it," she said to me. "But *come on*. You're the first one of us to have a boy actually *kiss* you. Don't leave us in suspense."

"I've been kissed before," Christina put in. Her gaze was studiously trained away from me. She was holding her left elbow behind her with her right hand, working on her shoulder flexibility before we moved over to the uneven bars.

Jessie was momentarily distracted. "When?" she asked. "You never told me about this."

Christina rolled her eyes. "I don't tell you *everything*," she said. "And it was last year, at Lindsay Barnes's birthday party. Carter kissed me during Spin the Bottle. It wasn't a big deal."

"That is so gross," Britt said. "I thought people only played that game in the movies."

"Maybe you're just not going to the right parties," Christina muttered. Even though she and Britt were on much better terms than they'd been when Britt first moved to Austin, Christina still got a little testy when she thought Britt was making fun of her. To be fair, Britt usually *was* making fun of her.

Jessie looked up from her piked position on the floor. "Focus, please!" she said. "Noelle, what is the story with you and David Schaeffer?"

I glanced at Scott, who was doing dips on the parallel bars at the other end of the gym. Even though there was no way he could hear our conversation from all the way over there, I still found myself lowering my voice. "I told you, there's nothing to tell. He just . . . thought we had a moment, I guess."

"I think it's kind of romantic," Jessie said.

"We were talking about books!" I blurted out. "How is that romantic?"

Christina and Jessie looked surprised by my outburst, but Britt just gave me an exasperated roll of the eyes. "Obviously, that was the only way he could connect with you," she said. "So, 'Do you agree that the movie version of *Bridge to Terabithia* ruined the spirit of the book?' is his way of saying, 'Hi, I think you're cute.'"

It wasn't the first time Britt's goofy sarcasm had left me completely unprepared for the truth of her words. This whole time, I'd been so caught up in how easy it was to talk to David that it hadn't occurred to me that maybe he had been choosing his words carefully to try to get closer to me. Now that I looked back on our conversations, it made some sense. And then I felt kind of bad, like maybe I'd led him to believe that I liked him back, when the whole time I'd simply been having a straightforward discussion with him about books.

Mo walked by. I put my head down and pretended like I was superintent on stretching. The last thing I wanted to do was get in trouble, especially since I'd gotten the feeling in the last week that Mo might have known more about our going to that dance than she was letting on, and that she might not be pleased about it. It was the kind of thing that she would never confront us about—technically, we were allowed to do what we wanted after we left the gym—but her disapproval could still be felt. We were allowed to go to dances, but as Elite gymnasts, we just weren't supposed to *want* to.

When warm-up time was over, we went to grab bars equipment from our gym bags. I looked up to see Scott approaching us.

"Hey," he said; I tried to figure out if his smile was directed at me personally or at the whole group. I wanted to pretend that it had been aimed in my direction, but there was nothing in his blue eyes to show that he was singling me out. And the other girls, the traitors, just giggled and smiled back at him. I hated to think how silly Scott must have found us.

"Hi, Noelle," he said, making my heart flutter. He *did* notice me! He hadn't said a special greeting to anyone else, and this time, he was definitely flashing his smile at me.

"Hi," I said, my voice squeaking, as I heard Britt stifle a laugh. I resisted the urge to nudge her in the ribs. "What's up?"

"I was thinking about you the other day," he said, and I felt my heart drop. "You said you had some questions about Junior Nationals, and I remembered one bit of advice I wanted to give you. I would definitely recommend flying in a day early, so you can get some rest and adjust to the time zone change. It also helps to have that extra time to get used to the equipment."

"Wow, thanks." True, it wasn't like he was confessing his undying love for me, but he had to know that Britt and Christina would probably qualify and would have questions, too, and yet he was directing his advice to me, not them. Maybe like how David had used books to try to connect with me, Scott was using this ruse of Junior Nationals. I got a thrill thinking that Scott, the same guy who'd effortlessly answered a reporter's questions with the kind of smooth, confident sound bites that ended up on television, might be nervous about starting up a conversation with *me*.

Scott wiped the sweat from the back of his neck with a towel. "No problem," he said. "Mo mentioned that your parents couldn't make the meeting last Friday, so she suggested that I might be able to help answer any questions."

If my heart had been flying somewhere above my head only a few moments before, it now crashed down to the ground. *Mo* was behind this? Scott hadn't chosen to talk to me at all. The reason he'd ignored Christina and Britt and addressed me specifically was because I was the only person whose parents hadn't attended the meeting.

"Oh, yeah," Christina said, turning her back on Scott. "My mom said that she'd like to arrange some kind of group dinner for when we're all in Philadelphia. You know, like where we all meet up at a nice restaurant."

Even if Scott had been put up to talking to me, I'd still wanted to prolong the encounter. But as soon as Christina closed him out of the conversation, he walked away. She hadn't really done anything wrong, but it made me suddenly furious at her.

I had only a few opportunities to show Scott how mature and interesting I could be, and she'd just ruined one of them. And didn't she get by now that her mother's idea of a "nice restaurant" was much different than my parents'? Her mother didn't work and devoted her entire life to shopping and monitoring Christina's gymnastics. Christina was her only child, and so of course she spared no expense—even hiring that stupid publicity coach so that Christina could give better interviews than the rest of us. My parents had five children and used to take us to the drive-in movie once a month as our only treat. They couldn't afford surf 'n' turf to celebrate, any more than they could afford to fly me to Philadelphia and have me stay extra days in the hotel just to get some rest.

Christina's smile was uncharacteristically gentle. "We could pay for you," she said. "Not a problem. My mom just wanted everyone to be able to celebrate after the competition."

"That's a little premature, don't you think?" I muttered. At first, she didn't respond, and so I thought she hadn't heard me, but then I looked up and she was staring at me, any tenderness gone.

"Excuse me?" she said. I'd heard Christina utter those words a thousand times, usually in a snide way, with the emphasis on the second syllable (ex*cuse* me?). But this time she sounded truly befuddled.

"You haven't even qualified to *go* to Junior Nationals yet," I said, "much less earned any reason to celebrate with a nice dinner. Don't you think you should just chill out?"

Now Britt and Jessie were staring at me, too. I knew that I was being horrible, and normally, I would've immediately apologized. *Normally,* I would've never said such hateful things in the first place. But I still felt that white-hot anger burning inside me, and, looking at their astonished faces, I suddenly didn't care that I had been mean.

"What?" I demanded.

But nobody answered me. Instead, Christina turned to Britt and said, "Well. I guess we should get to work if we want to actually make it to the competition."

"Yeah," Britt agreed. "We need a lot of practice if we're going to have that celebratory dinner."

Christina stalked over to the uneven bars, with Britt at her heels. I remembered that it wasn't too long ago that Christina and I were inseparable and Britt was the outsider. Not that I wanted it to be like that still, but I felt a pang as I watched them walk away.

Jessie put her hand on my shoulder, her green eyes dark with concern. "Noelle," she said tentatively, "is everything okay?"

In a different mood, I could've almost laughed. No, everything was *not* okay. I had a problem that had no real solution—either I told my parents about Junior Nationals and let them pay for me to go, even if it meant that we lost our house and the store and everything my parents had worked for, or I kept my mouth shut and risked being left behind.

Jessie was still waiting for an answer; I resisted the urge to shrug her hand away. "Everything's fine," I said. "I'm just tired, that's all."

She gave my shoulder a squeeze. "I know you get stressed about big competitions," she said. "But if anyone can do it, you can. You're good, Noelle. You know you're going to rock it."

If I had allowed myself to be completely honest, with no false humility, I would have admitted that Jessie was right. I had complete faith in my abilities. It was everything else that I had a hard time believing in. I used to buy in to all that stuff about how the most important thing was to do your best, but there were some situations where that just wasn't enough.

I didn't know what I was supposed to do.

Eight

By the time I got home that night, my words to Jessie weren't just an excuse. I really was tired, and cranky, and all I wanted to do was throw myself onto my bed and lie there on my stomach until I fell asleep. Even taking off my clothes first seemed like too much to deal with by that point.

But when I walked through the front door of our apartment upstairs, Radu was sitting on the couch, and he shook his head at me.

"What?" I asked. The serious expression on his face scared me. I couldn't remember the last time I'd seen it—maybe not since Papu's stroke. My first thought was that the bank was there to take everything away.

He put his finger to his lips and gestured to me to come join him on the couch. "Mihai's in big trouble," he whispered.

And then I heard it—the walls of the apartment weren't that thick, and Mama's voice cut right through them.

"How could you?" she was saying, at a decibel level usually reserved for when the twins were trying to play with electrical sockets. "We trusted you! We may not have been happy about you skipping out on your shifts at the store, but we figured it was just a phase, that you'd come back around when you were ready."

There was a pause, and then her voice came again, only louder this time. "It *is* a big deal!" she yelled. "You could've gone to jail. Do you realize that?"

I raised my eyebrows. "What did he do?" I whispered to Radu. Had he been busted for trespassing on that empty lot behind the store? It made me shudder to think that I could've been caught for the very same thing only a few days before, but it also seemed like a relatively minor offense. Of course it wasn't our property, but it wasn't like any-one else ever used it, and Mihai went there to reflect on things sometimes. Where was the harm in that?

"He got brought home by a cop for trying to buy cigarettes with a fake ID," Radu whispered back. "Now, be quiet; I'm trying to hear Tata."

Then it was worse than I had thought. I'd kind of known that Mihai was smoking, from the stale smell on his clothes, but it was still jarring to get such clear confirmation. I didn't get what would make him take up such a disgusting habit. I remem-bered that back in elementary school, a traveling troupe had done a show in our gym about the dan-gers of drugs and alcohol. I'd only been in second grade, but Mihai and Radu had been old enough to go to the performance. They'd both signed a pledge right there and then, promising not to make bad choices. I wondered if Radu remembered that. It appeared that Mihai didn't.

There was a lower-pitched rumbling through the wall that was obviously Tata's voice, but I couldn't make out the words. He seldom raised his voice; he didn't need to. With a disappointed look or a shake of the head, he could make you feel ten times worse than Mama could, even after all her yelling.

I bit my lip, torn between feeling there was something wrong with listening in on one of my brother's worst moments and not wanting to miss a single word. Then Mama started in on him again. I stayed frozen.

"You're grounded, do you understand me? You'll go to summer school, come home, work in the store, and spend time with the family. That's *it*."

Our parents almost never grounded us, so this was yet another sign of just how much trouble Mihai was really in. It wasn't that Mama and Tata were so lenient; it was more that we never usually gave them any cause to take such drastic measures. The last time any of us had been punished to that extent, it was Radu, when he left to go swimming in the lake with his friend and didn't tell anyone. That time, I was pretty sure my parents grounded him not only to teach him a lesson, but because they didn't know how to handle how scared they felt. Maybe now with Mihai, it was a similar situation.

As if Mama had read my mind, she said, "You know I hate that it comes to this, but you leave me no choice. I'm not going to search your room for stashed cigarettes, but I'm trusting you when you say you don't have any. If I find out that you're still smoking, I'll look in every drawer and under your bed. Got it?"

My parents never invaded our privacy. Christina used to write in a diary, and her mom always "happened" to find it while she was putting Christina's laundry away. I had pointed out to her that maybe she should start doing her own laundry, but instead she'd just stopped keeping a journal. She said that there wasn't a lot in there, anyway—mostly just embarrassing stuff about what boy she liked. The biggest thing that had gotten her in trouble was complaints about her mother. Apparently she'd once written something about hating her mother's empanadas that Mrs. Flores read and took really personally.

The door to my parents' bedroom opened, making Radu and me both jump. Tata didn't even look at us as he crossed the living room and headed back downstairs to the store. It was closed, so I knew Tata was going down there to get a little space. Sometimes, when he needed to think, he would shut himself in the office and "go over the books." That was how you knew he had something on his mind, because Mama *always* took care of the accounting for the store, and she complained bitterly if Tata tried to touch it. She said she spent more time undoing his mistakes than balancing the accounts in the first place.

The next person out of the bedroom was Mama, who gave Radu and me a disapproving look as she went to the kitchen. But that was nothing compared to Mihai's scowl as he finally emerged from the room.

"Don't you have anything better to do?" he asked Radu.

Radu just smirked. "Not really, no. And it sounds like you won't have much else to do, either. Enjoy house arrest."

Mihai reached over to slap the side of Radu's head, but he was grinning. That was the thing about the two of them—they fought all the time, but they also made up quickly. Since they were only a year apart, Mihai and Radu had always shared a special closeness. They had each other, Mama had Tata, and the twins would no doubt grow up in their own little world. Sometimes I felt like the only one without a partner.

As if on cue, Mihai finally acknowledged my presence. "Hey, isn't it past your bedtime?" he asked.

It was true that most nights when I had late

practice, I came home, ate a little dinner, and then pretty much collapsed into bed. In fact, that had been my plan earlier. But for some reason, I didn't like the reminder. It emphasized the fact that I really didn't have a life outside of gymnastics.

"I was just leaving," I muttered, pushing up from the couch.

Mihai ran his fingers through his hair. "Hey," he said. "Noelle, come on."

He called after me again as I headed for my room, but I pretended not to hear. Instead I closed my door and fell onto my bed on my stomach. My face was mashed into the covers, and I could feel the wetness of my own breath on my cheeks and nose, but I didn't care.

Gymnastics *was* my whole life, which meant that if I didn't go to Nationals . . . I'd have nothing. I still didn't want to have to ask my parents for the money, but there had to be *some* way to make it happen.

It wasn't even two days after Mama and Tata's big talk with Mihai that he skipped out on his first Saturday shift at the store. As soon as I got home from a half day of practice, I had put on some disposable latex gloves and joined Tata in packaging soups and salads for sale.

"He's probably just hanging out with his friends," I said, stealing a glance at Tata's tight face. Radu had said that Tata had been livid when he'd found Mihai gone that morning, although his was a simmering anger. Mama's bad moods usually manifested themselves in her slamming things and muttering to herself, but when Tata got mad he got really quiet, as though he couldn't trust himself to say anything at all. In some ways, his were worse.

Now, Tata only grunted. I realized that he probably placed some of the blame for Mihai's behavior on those faceless friends who were terrible influences. "He might be studying for his geometry summer school class," I said. "I heard it was really hard."

"Don't make excuses for him," Tata said, so low I almost didn't catch it. "I don't know my son. He can look us in the face and say one thing and then do another."

That day when Mihai and I had talked in the clearing, I had wished I'd thought to ask him what was going on with *him*. I'd been so focused on my own problems that I hadn't even checked to see if everything was okay in his life. It was one thing to sneak out and start smoking, but to disobey our parents so blatantly after they'd talked to him was unlike my brother. We'd always been brought up to have more respect than that.

Tata wiped his hands on a dish towel before rumpling my hair. "You don't need to concern yourself with this," he said. "You've always been the easy one, the one your mother and I didn't have to worry about."

I wanted to tell him that he didn't need to worry about Mihai, either, that everything would turn out all right. But I wasn't sure anymore myself. Instead, I smiled, reaching for the aubergines to peel for our specialty salad. Their purple skin was soft from boiling, and I enjoyed the familiar feel of it underneath my fingernails.

"How is gymnastics?" he asked. "It's been a while since you've told me what's new."

"Oh." I wanted to tell him about my new dismount on beam, but if I did, there was a chance that he'd ask why we were adding it, and then I would have to lie outright about the National Championships. "Not much. Practice, practice, practice. You know."

"You still having fun?" he asked sternly, as

though there would be punishment if I said I wasn't.

I nodded and smiled, although I didn't look up from peeling the aubergines. I reached for the special wooden knife to cut them up. Mama had taught me that using a metal knife would give the eggplant a weird flavor, and she always said it was attention to detail that made things go from good to great.

That was a lesson that I'd carried with me my whole life, from school to gymnastics. It was why I always pointed my toes, fanned out my fingers, and kept my knees together. Any one of those things might have meant only a tenth of a point here or there, but when you put them together, they made your whole presentation crisp and beautiful.

"We're so proud of you for qualifying for Nationals," Tata said. "Aren't they soon?"

I froze. How could I answer that question without lying? Or revealing more than I wanted to?

"Um . . ." I began, but then Radu popped his head in the doorway.

"Hey, Noelle," he said. "Your boyfriend's here asking about you."

Tata shot me a startled look, and I felt heat crawl up from my neck to the tips of my ears. "Scott?" I asked, my voice shaking. "He's not my boyfriend."

I tried to say it casually, as though it had never occurred to me even to *want* Scott as my boyfriend. But it was hard to stop my hands from trembling. What could Scott be doing here? Did this mean that maybe he did think of me, at least a little bit?

"Scott?" Radu repeated. "He said his name was David. How many boyfriends do you have?"

"Just one," I said, then hastily corrected myself. "I mean, none. I don't have a boyfriend. David's a boy, and he's my friend, but . . ."

Tata and Radu were both staring at me now as I peeled off my latex gloves. "I'll see what he wants," I muttered.

David was standing out front drumming his fingers on the counter. He straightened when he saw me approach.

"Hey, Noelle," he said. "Wow, you look . . . great."

Considering that I was wearing cutoff jean shorts and an old shirt that Mihai had tie-dyed back when he was eight years old (yeah, and it still fit me now—the joys of being small), I knew David must be lying. I tugged self-consciously at the hem of my shorts.

"Uh, thanks."

Radu and Tata had joined us out front and

were sorting random items at the other end of the counter in the most obvious way possible. I grimaced at Radu, but he just wiggled his eyebrows back at me.

"Let's go outside," I said, the words coming out more clipped than I had intended.

It was a dry, hot day, and the sun overhead was unrelenting. I led David to a shady spot under a tree, but even then I could feel the heat seep through my shirt, as if we were in a sauna.

"What are you doing here?" I asked.

"I'm sorry," he said. "I can't seem to get anything right. I came here to apologize for the other night, but I guess I should've called first."

Maybe it was the heat, but I felt some of my tension melt away hearing that. As awkward as David's kiss had been, part of me didn't want him apologizing for it. I couldn't explain why, but there it was. "It's okay," I said. "I'm sorry I ran out like that."

"No, I shouldn't have . . ." David's face went red, and it wasn't from the sun. "You know. . . . Sorry."

I leaned back against the tree, but I couldn't meet his gaze. "It's okay," I repeated.

And then suddenly, David was talking quickly,

his words tripping over one another. "I've liked you for a while. But you probably knew that—it was so obvious. You're amazing, the way you're so smart and pretty and easy to talk to, and I think it's really cool that you're a gymnast. I'm the most uncoordinated person in the world, so I can't even imagine doing what you do."

"Sometimes *I* can't imagine doing what I do," I said ruefully.

David kicked at a tree root, loosening some dirt from the bark with the toe of his sneaker. "So . . . what do you think? Would you go out with me? We could go to the movies, or to the carnival. Whatever you feel like."

It all seemed too surreal. I couldn't believe I was standing there, my hair pulled back in a sloppy ponytail that probably left hundreds of flyaways around my face, wearing this stupid shirt, and a boy was asking me out. For some reason, it was a scenario that I had never pictured actually happening to me.

Or maybe I had, and it was just the wrong boy.

"I don't know," I said. I hated the way David's smile faltered. It wasn't that I wanted to hurt him, and I tried to think of an excuse that would make him understand. "Like you said, I'm a gymnast. And unfortunately, this is the big competitive season right now. I can't afford to lose focus."

He was still looking at me as though I'd kicked his puppy. "Oh."

"It's nothing against you," I said. "But Junior National Championships are coming up, and I have to concentrate on that."

I wondered what David would think if the competition rolled around and I wasn't there, but then I told myself to stop being so paranoid. He probably would've forgotten all about me by then, and there was no way he was going to follow a gymnastics competition just because he'd once liked a girl who might be competing in it.

Besides, I would find a way to be there. I had to.

Then again, David seemed to have other ideas. "But after that," he said, "when school starts back up . . . You might have a different answer?"

By then, I hoped that maybe Scott and I would have had a chance to get closer. After all, we had the whole rest of the summer to train together, and even if Scott *was* put up to talking to me by the coach, at least that was something.

But of course, I couldn't say any of this to David.

It wasn't that I wanted to lead him on; I just couldn't stand to see him crushed.

"Maybe," I said.

He grinned, and this time it reached his amber-colored eyes. "I'll take it," he said. "So here's where I guess I wish you good luck in your competition?"

I thought I'd been handling this the smoothest way possible, but suddenly I wondered if I'd only made a complicated situation even more so. "I guess," I said.

"Good luck," he said. "Not that you need it."

At this point, I didn't know what I needed, although a time machine might have come in handy. Then I could have rewound to the day that Mo handed me that envelope about the championships, and this time I might tell my parents about it right away. I could have rewound back to before the man came about the foreclosure and figured out a way to prevent that from happening. I could have rewound back to when I was a five-year-old who just loved gymnastics and had nothing to worry about except whether I'd ever get the momentum to kick my legs over my head and execute a perfect back walkover, a move I could do now in my sleep.

Nine

I did end up going to the carnival, just not with David. The next Sunday we had off, Mrs. Flores dropped us all at the gates with instructions to call if we needed anything. Mama had given me a twenty-dollar bill that morning, which I'd tried to refuse.

"Take it," she'd said. "I know it will only buy you a couple of rides and a corn dog. I wish I could give you more, but we have to put in our supply orders today."

"But the house—" I started to say, but Mama's lips tightened.

"You let me worry about that," she said. "If I

can't spare a little money for my daughter to have fun, well . . ." I waited for the end of that sentence, but it didn't come.

I was so tired of feeling guilty, so sick of this pattern, that I just took the money. Sometimes I hated the fact that I was a huge drain on the family, what with the expense of my gymnastics training and all of the stuff that went with it, and then other times I felt like I was the only one of the kids who cared about our family's situation. Radu would've taken the twenty and whined for more. The twins would've cried until they got what they wanted. At the rate Mihai was going, he probably would've stolen the twenty from Mama's purse.

Maybe that wasn't fair. But even after Mihai had gotten yelled at—*again*—for slacking off on his responsibilities at the store and not coming home by curfew, he seemed only to sink further into his own juvenile-delinquent world. I had begun to wonder if I'd imagined that conversation we'd had in the woods behind the store.

Britt insisted that we head to the Ferris wheel first. I'd always been kind of a wimp about the Ferris wheel. I hated the uncertainty of that moment when the momentum stopped, suspending you in midair while more people boarded the ride. It always seemed like I got stuck at the very top when that happened. I could fly off a bar eight feet in the air and trust that I was going to catch it again, but I felt all fluttery about sitting in a totally encased and completely safe box with my three closest friends. Another example of one of those weird personality conundrums you faced as a gymnast.

I swallowed my doubts and climbed into the Ferris wheel car with Christina, Britt, and Jessie. The ride operator closed the door behind us, and I felt a lurch in my stomach as the wheel swayed into motion.

Jessie had been rambling on about her father, and she didn't skip a beat as we started our ascent. "We'll go camping the weekend that you guys are at Nationals," she said. "Since it's not like I'm eligible to compete anyway, it's perfect timing."

"Yeah," I said. "The timing of everything just couldn't be better."

It wasn't surprising that no one seemed to get the irony in my tone, since I was almost never sarcastic, but it was annoying. I turned to stare out of the Ferris wheel car, pressing my lips together before I could say anything else. I'd been in a bad mood since that morning, and I knew if I didn't clear my head the entire day would be ruined.

Of course, the best way to clear my head was possibly *not* to look down and realize just how high up we were. From this vantage point, I could look out over the entire carnival, from the Tilt-a-Whirl to the concession stands, surrounded by crowded picnic tables. Almost directly below us, I saw a toddler holding a stuffed panda bear that was bigger than she was.

I tried to look away, but my eyes kept seeking confirmation of how high off the ground we were, as though I needed to be reminded. I turned to glance at the ground behind me, and that was when I saw them.

Scott was at the carnival. With a girl. She had dark, curly hair, and even from this distance I could see that she was smiling. He was buying her pink cotton candy from a vendor, presenting it to her with an exaggerated flourish.

My completely irrational fear of the Ferris wheel had been that there'd be some horrific accident, while my more reasonable worry had been that I would get one glimpse of the ground a hundred feet below me and pass out. Now I was more concerned that I would throw up. If Scott leaned in for a kiss with his mystery girl, this was a very distinct possibility.

"So, Christina," Britt said, pointing an invisible microphone in Christina's direction. "Your public is dying to know—what is your favorite ride?"

Once Britt had found out about Christina's media coach, she'd teased her every chance she got by pretending to interview her. It was getting kind of old, but Christina seemed to relish any opportunity to practice what she'd say, even if it was because Britt was making fun of her.

Christina flipped her long, dark hair behind her shoulder and pretended to think about the question. "That's tough," she said. "Each ride is fun in its own way. I don't think I could pick just one."

Jessie frowned. "But I thought you liked the carousel."

I craned my neck to try to find Scott and his date, but they had disappeared. The funhouse was right next to the cotton-candy stand, and I imagined them stumbling toward a dark corner where they could be alone.

Britt continued with her fake interview. "We know you're very busy, but one more question before you go. What's your take on the carnival? Is it a ridiculous waste of time and money, or good clean fun?"

Christina gave Britt a wide smile that showed off her beautiful white teeth. Maybe I was imagining it, but it seemed as if Mrs. Flores might also have sprung for some whitening strips when she paid for the publicity coach. "The carnival is what you make of it," she said in an overly bright voice. "Me, I choose to make it a positive experience to enjoy with my friends."

Jessie wrinkled her nose. "What kind of response is *that*?"

"A noncommittal one," Christina said. I could tell by the way she enunciated *noncommittal* that it was a direct quote from her publicity coach. "The trick is to answer every question in a vague, middle-of-the-road way that makes you look good and doesn't give them any sound bites they could take out of context."

Britt dropped her fake reporter act. "It kind of makes you sound like you're just an idiot who didn't understand the question."

"No, you don't get it." Christina sighed, as though this were the thousandth time she'd explained this, when really it was the first any of us was hearing about it. "Say a reporter asks you if you're going to Nationals. How would you respond?"

"I'd say I hoped to qualify for Elite later this summer," Jessie said, "but that I wouldn't be Elite in time to go to Nationals."

"And that's the wrong way to handle it."

Jessie furrowed her brow. "Why? It's the truth."

"Because it only reminds everyone that you're not Elite yet," Christina explained. "You should be crossing your fingers that that little tidbit of information wouldn't come up at all in the interview. You definitely shouldn't bring it up yourself. Instead, you say something about how this year you'll be rooting for your teammates, and you can't wait to join them on the floor next year."

The Ferris wheel had stopped to let on new riders, and just my luck, we were stuck at the top. *Someone* had to be in the car that stopped toward the bottom, or halfway up, but for whatever reason, it was like the carnival gods knew that I dreaded this moment, and now they were cackling away as they froze my car at the highest point.

To make matters worse, Britt had started to rock back and forth next to me in her seat. I closed my eyes, the car swaying with each movement.

"That's stupid," Britt said, as though she hadn't been in the middle of giving me a panic attack. "What you said is basically the same as Jessie's answer."

"That's the beauty of it," Christina said. "It's not. Jessie admitted that she wasn't a member of the Elite team yet, and then she said she *hoped* to be there next year, both of which make her seem insecure."

"Better than being cocky," Jessie muttered, in a tone that made it clear she thought Christina was acting a little full of herself.

"That's why I *said* you have to go middle of the road," Christina shot back. I opened my eyes just in time to see her throw her hands up in the air. The Ferris wheel car was still rocking. "Obviously, none of us knows for sure if we'll make it to Junior Nationals or not, or how well we'll do."

Britt had one hand on the pole that connected the bottom of the car to the roof, and there was a sharp squeal from an un-oiled joint somewhere as she continued to use the force of her body to move the car. I reached over to still her, but the sound of my hand slapping her bare knee was a lot louder in the confined space than I'd expected.

"Stop," I said, my voice low.

Normally, Britt would have continued to push it, but something must've told her I was serious, because she raised her eyebrows, but immediately quit moving. "Okaaay," she said, drawing the word out to make it sound like *I* was the unreasonable one.

"God, Noelle, don't be so touchy," Christina said. "As you so kindly pointed out, *you* don't need to worry. You could tell a reporter you've earned an invitation to the Nationals without even being arrogant. And everyone knows you'd have to break a leg not to earn a medal."

"Thank you," I said, and this time there was no hiding my snarky tone. "I can't tell you how privileged it makes me feel to benefit from your wisdom. Who needs a publicity coach when they have friends who know everything?"

Christina gaped at me. Britt made a show of rubbing her knee where I'd slapped it, and Jessie carefully turned her eyes toward the view outside the car, as though she'd rather have been reminded of the huge distance we had between us and the ground than meet my gaze.

I just closed my eyes again as I felt the ride

lurch back into motion, hoping that next time, we'd be getting off.

The rest of the day at the carnival, I kept my eyes peeled for Scott and his girlfriend, but as much as I dreaded running into them, I wasn't prepared for the person I saw instead.

The first thing Christina said to me after the tension on the Ferris wheel was "Hey, isn't that your brother?"

I glanced over in the direction she was pointing in, and sure enough, it was Mihai. He was wearing a white collared shirt with a picture of a red tent on the back that looked like it belonged at the circus instead of the carnival. He was breaking down boxes and shoving them into a Dumpster. As we watched, he stopped to wipe sweat off his forehead, surveying the piles of boxes he had left.

"Mihai?"

He spun around at the sound of my voice, his eyes shadowed with some unknown emotion for a second before he scowled at me. "What are *you* doing here?"

I glanced meaningfully at the row of booths set up with various games—toss a ball into a cup of water to win a goldfish, hit a balloon with a dart and win an airbrushed picture of a wolf howling at the moon with a castle in the background. "Obviously, I'm here with my friends. Having fun. You know, a totally normal thing to be doing at a carnival."

Mihai waved halfheartedly at my friends. "Hey, guys."

"Do you work here?" Christina asked, even though it said so right across the front of his shirt.

I didn't give him a moment to answer before cutting in. "Do Mama and Tata know about this?"

Mihai grabbed me by the upper arm and led me away from my group. Unfortunately, that also meant that we were standing closer to the Dumpster. I wrinkled my nose at the stench of rotting concession food.

"No, they don't," he hissed. "And they *can't.*"

"But you're missing your shifts at the store," I sputtered. "You're breaking curfew. Mama and Tata are already mad, and what about your grades in summer school? You failed geometry once; are you really going to fail it again because you're skipping class to pick up trash?"

"You let me worry about that," he said. "This is just temporary, okay? I know it's grunt work, but for the month the carnival is in town, they're paying me pretty well to do it. Please . . . don't tell Mama and Tata."

I bit my lip. "You're not using the money to buy cigarettes, are you? Or to do anything else that's bad?"

"Believe me," he said. "That is not what this is about. I quit smoking, not that I really did it that much in the first place—I just started it to impress some friends. It was stupid."

My gaze flicked back to Jessie, Britt, and Christina, who made no attempt to hide the fact that they'd been watching the whole exchange. Britt raised her eyebrows and gestured as if to say, *Well?*

I turned back to Mihai. "Okay," I said. "I won't tell. But promise me that you've got a good reason for lying to them."

He looked me in the eyes. "Do you have a good reason for lying about Junior Nationals?"

I wanted to protest that I wasn't *lying* so much as not telling, but he had a point. "I thought I did," I said.

"Then so do I," he said. "Now, I have to get back to work. You go enjoy the carnival with your friends."

The girls said their good-byes to my brother, and as we walked away, Christina and Jessie were all atwitter about running into him. Britt just wanted to know what we were going to do next, but Christina couldn't believe I hadn't known about Mihai's job.

"He's my older brother, not my confidant," I said irritably.

"I just thought that your family was, like . . . tight. You all work in the store, and whenever there's a birthday or a third cousin graduates, there's a huge party."

I'd been friends with Christina for five years, and she'd always had her insensitive moments. She didn't mean to, but she spoke her mind, and sometimes what came out of her mouth sounded harsh. But couldn't she see that she was *not* helping? Maybe my family had been close once, but now . . . who knew? I was lying to my parents (by omission, mostly, but still), Mihai was lying to my parents, I was lying to my parents for Mihai. It was all such a mess.

Maybe, I thought, I could get a job at the carnival, and pay for my competition that way. But there was no way I'd earn enough in time, and then it would just mean more lies and more secrets.

I felt a familiar heat rising in my body. It was like the sensation I had when I was out on the competition floor, sprinting toward the vaulting horse and about to launch myself ten feet in the air—the adrenaline, the pent-up aggression. Only this time, there was nothing to channel it into. It was just there, this swirl of hot anger running through me like a current.

"How about bumper cars?" I suggested.

Ten

For the next week, things were a little tense in the gym. Part of it was due to the upcoming competitions—which was totally natural—but it wasn't just that. Jessie was still irritated with Britt, because Britt had repeatedly banged her bumper car into Jessie's at the carnival. "It's not called 'gently touching cars,'" Britt had pointed out when Jessie yelled at her. It was a stupid argument, but Jessie was so wound up about the upcoming camping trip with her father that she seemed extra sensitive.

Then there was Christina, who was holding a grudge against me. A month earlier, I probably would've just apologized for any hurtful comments and moved on. But now, I was determined that I wouldn't be the one to budge. I'd only spoken the truth, after all. Christina *was* getting ahead of herself, talking about what she'd say to a reporter about Nationals and making assumptions about who was going and who wasn't. It wasn't fair that she was allowed to say whatever she wanted, but I didn't have the same privilege. It wasn't all about her.

And that was why I was upset: Christina was so busy worrying about herself that she didn't even seem to notice that her supposed best friend was dealing with her own insecurities.

So when Parents' Day at the gym rolled around, the four of us were hardly feeling like a cohesive team. Parents' Day was held every year and was a chance for all the gymnasts—from those in the toddler tumbling class to the members of the Elite squad—to showcase what we were working on. We would all preview parts of our competitive routines for the parents, but the highlight would be the group exhibition, where we performed a synchronized dance with the younger girls and took turns tumbling across the floor. It was practically the same every year, but people always got a kick out of seeing one of us unfurl a double twist only to be followed by a four-year-old attempting a cart-wheel.

The younger classes were showing off their skills while we were in the locker room, having just changed into our Parents' Day exhibition leotards, with sequins in the shape of a *V* across the chest. They wouldn't have seemed so tacky if it weren't for the fact that we all had to wear them. There was some strange phenomenon that made it okay for our outfits to match when it came to competing at the World Championships or something, but kind of cheesy when it was only for your parents.

"Why doesn't Mo just put a ruffled collar around our necks and make us dance around on our hind legs?" Britt muttered, pulling the shiny purple fabric of her leotard away from her stomach.

"We *are* dancing on our hind legs," Jessie said. "What other legs do we have?"

Britt rolled her eyes. "Obviously, I'm making a reference to those dogs at the circus, not that I would expect you to get it. And technically, we don't have *hind* legs, we just have legs."

"Well, why not say we have to jump through

hoops, then?" Jessie snapped. "Wouldn't that be a better joke?"

"Because jumping through hoops is kind of cool," Britt said. "But have you ever seen dogs dancing on their back legs? It's sad. It's worse than sad—it's abuse, like this exhibition dance."

Christina broke in with a guttural sound of frustration. "For the love of Mary Lou Retton, would you shut up? This is the stupidest argument I've ever heard in my life."

I couldn't have agreed more, but I wasn't about to admit that to Christina, given that I was still mad at her. Instead, I stepped out into the hallway and peeked around the wall. The Level Fives were standing in rows on the floor mat, their feet on the lines where pieces of the blue carpet joined. They were executing slow, deliberate back walkovers, trying to stay straight.

My eyes skipped to the wooden bleachers against one wall. Mrs. Flores was there, sitting in the very bottom row, chatting with other gym mothers, including Jessie's mom. Britt's mom wasn't there yet, but she'd promised Britt she was on her way and would arrive by the time we took the floor. Britt's mom owned a day care center, and so she was often running late, because of some spit-up emergency or parent meeting or whatever else.

Tata was still back at the store, but Mama was sitting two rows up from Mrs. Flores and Jessie's mom, at the very top of the bleachers. She'd brought the twins with her, and Cristian was squirming to get off her lap while Costel rhythmically banged his favorite Matchbox car against the padded seat. She looked a little harried, as she often did when she was out with the twins, but she was smiling at the gymnasts on the floor.

I only hoped that she would be too distracted by the twins to get a chance to really talk to Mo. Mama had asked me about Nationals just a few days before, but luckily she'd had so much other stuff going on that it had been pretty easy to change the subject and get her thinking about something else. My go-to subject to ask about was what was going to happen about the house and the store, which brought that closed-off look to Mama's eyes and made me feel like a complete jerk for bringing it up, but it was also the only subject guaranteed to make Mama forget about gymnastics.

Mama had been a gymnast back in Romania, until a back injury had stopped her from getting much further than the level I was at now. On the internet, I'd been able to find a very grainy version of her beam routine from the European Championships held in the 1980s. I used to watch it ten times a day. I even sent a message to the person who'd posted it, asking if she had any other footage from the Romanian team during those years, but I'd never heard back. When I showed the clip to Mama, she'd watched it silently with shining eyes. Whether she was crying from nostalgia or regret, I didn't know.

You'd think that all of this would have meant that Mama would be the typical sports parent, trying to live her dreams through her kid, but it really wasn't like that. Mama understood all the work gymnastics took, and she wanted me to learn the discipline of the sport, but she also wanted to make sure I was having fun. She'd admitted to me once that it wasn't always fun back in Romania, where they took gymnastics very seriously and where there were girls lined up to take your place if you stopped working hard enough or if you got hurt. Sometimes I wondered if Mama would rather I be one of the Level Five girls, whose biggest aspirations were a blue ribbon at a gym-hosted invitational.

She stood up, finally letting the squirming Cristian out of her arms, and waved to someone. I turned to follow her gaze and saw Mihai and Radu come in through the entrance.

The Level Five girls finished their part of the exhibition, and I retreated back into the locker room before my family saw me. There was no way to keep Parents' Day a secret from my mother, since she had gone every year, so my only concern was keeping my mother away from Mo and the other parents. Considering that Mo always made it a point to tell our parents how well we were doing, this seemed almost impossible. Short of pulling the fire alarm, I couldn't think of any way to do it.

My eyes went to the tempting red square on the wall that said PULL DOWN in big letters. If Britt had been in my position, she would totally have done it, without a second thought. I wasn't Britt, but I was starting to wish I'd shared my problems with the other girls so I could have gotten their insights right now.

"I've seen you do the Electric Slide," Britt was saying to Jessie, making an exaggerated step to her right, complete with sarcastic jazz hands.

Maybe I could fake having hurt my wrist or

something. Not enough to have to miss practice, but just enough to have to stay off it today and go home immediately afterward. But then Mo would definitely talk to my mother, to make sure I was icing it and wrapping it and all that.

The Level Five girls filed into the locker room, which was our cue to take our places on the floor. Jessie stuck her tongue out one last time at Britt, who didn't have time to respond before Christina shoved her toward the door.

"Come on, guys," Christina said. "Let's just get this over with. We'll do our little dance and routines, the parents can coo over the tots doing their thing, and then we can go back to being competitive Elite gymnasts."

Since she was the shortest, Britt led us out, to the sound of our parents' applause; then I went, followed by Jessie and Christina. The toddlers in the tumbling class were waiting for us in their starting positions on the floor, which were supposed to be straddle splits. Instead, it just looked like they were sitting with their legs a little wider open than usual. I had been faking a smile up until that point, but I couldn't help biting back a grin at the image. I remembered the days when I'd been that proud to show off my split to my parents, when I wasn't even able to get all the way down on the floor yet.

I sought out my family in the bleachers, and my mother picked up Cristian's hand and waved it at me. Radu made a goofy face, and Mihai smiled, although I could tell even from this distance that his eyes were serious. I knew he was probably thinking about his job and my competition and all the other secrets that we had between us at that point. At least, those were the things I was thinking about.

And it was right then that I let go. It was too late for me to compete at Nationals now; the competition was in just under two months, and the deadline to register at the special rate for one of the hotel rooms was coming up sooner than that.

The music started—some horrible medley that included a dance remix of a popular pop-country ballad about reaching for your dreams—and I took the arm of one of the toddlers to help her to a standing position. After that, the Elite girls were each supposed to do a back handspring while the little girls did backward somersaults, but my toddler's was more sideways, and so I had to break out of formation to lead her back to the group.

That was pretty much how it went for the rest

of the routine. I spent more time chasing after one of the toddlers than I did on the actual choreographed dance, but that was the point of the whole ordeal, anyway. Parents didn't come to watch a perfect performance from the Elite girls; they came to marvel at tiny, adorable children with hair in pigtails who didn't know a cartwheel from a round-off.

The CD being piped over the loudspeakers played the last strident note of the mix as we hit our last pose with a flourish. Or at least, the Elite girls did. The tumbling toddlers mostly staggered into a position closely resembling ours, beaming up at their proud parents in the audience and waving even when they weren't supposed to. I caught Christina's eye, and I knew in that moment that we were all united: we were just glad the humiliation was over.

I looked back at the bleachers again; I was half expecting to see my mother chatting with Mrs. Flores and Jessie's mom, comparing notes. But when my gaze reached the top row, she was gone. Only Mihai remained, his hands in his pockets. I broke away from the other girls, ignoring the music that had started up to signify the final showcase event. I was supposed to be out there on the floor for that.

We all were, even Scott, although his parents weren't there, since he was eighteen and almost in college and didn't need his parents to come to things like this. He'd smiled at me earlier, but I hadn't been able to look at him without thinking about him buying cotton candy for his mystery girl.

I climbed the bleachers, searching Mihai's face for any clues. Had Mama found out about my big lie? I wasn't stupid. If she'd had to hear about the biggest competition of my career from someone else's mom or my coach, she'd have felt like an idiot. She'd be hurt. She'd be angry.

"What's going on?" I asked. I didn't need to spell it out; Mihai knew what I meant.

"Mama had to leave," he said. "Costel said that he had to use the bathroom, and Radu said he'd take him, but then Costel said it was like the time we went to the zoo, and you know what that means, so . . ."

"Ugh, TMI," I said.

Mihai grinned. "Nothing like a little diarrhea to really break up a party, huh?"

"Don't even say that word," I said. "I am totally grossed out right now."

"And totally relieved?"

Of course, he would know that Mama's leaving early meant that she hadn't had a chance to talk to the other parents or to Mo, who was over by the beam helping Level Fours show off some of their skills for the grand finale. Cheng was nowhere to be found, but then, he usually avoided these kind of events. With Cheng, it was like he only had twenty words to say on any given day; he didn't like to waste them on small talk with parents. Instead, he used them up in saying things like, "Again!" or "Tighter! Higher!"

"Yeah," I said. "And relieved."

Mihai gestured toward the floor. "Are you supposed to be participating in this?"

"Technically. But I'm really not feeling it."

"Good," he said. "Neither am I. Let's go grab some fries at the concession stand—sorry, apple slices for you or whatever else you gymnasts eat— and we'll wait out the explosive diarrhea outbreak."

"*Mihai!* Seriously, you're going to make me sick."

We headed down through the bleachers and around the floor mat to the exit. I caught Mo's frown, but I knew that there was nothing she could do to stop me as long as she was spotting the Level

Fours. My rebellion wasn't quite the same as pulling the fire alarm, but it felt good. It was like letting some of the air out of that angry balloon of energy that had been sitting in the pit of my stomach for what felt like a long time.

But it didn't make it go away completely. I realized that it was true, what I'd told Mihai. Obviously I *was* relieved to have my secret still intact. And yet, as much as I'd dreaded her reaction, a part of me *wanted* Mama to know the truth. The weight of this whole deception was still on me, and until it lifted, there could be no relief.

Eleven

"**Y**ou're not setting up," Mo said after my tenth rep of my beam dismount. "You need more power in back handspring."

Of course, Mo was right. I wasn't getting enough momentum with my round-off to back handspring on the beam, which meant that I wasn't setting up the full-twisting double back dismount properly. Because I wasn't getting the height on the move, my landings were piked, my body bent at the waist, throwing my balance off. Every single time, I was forced to take a small step forward.

"Try again," she said. "This time, do like you on floor."

Beam was usually my best event, and I prided myself on being able to flip on the four-inch-wide surface as though I was frolicking on the floor mat. But for some reason, today it wasn't coming together.

I climbed back up on the beam, taking my position at the very end. I always touched one pointed foot to the back of the beam, just to be sure that I was as far as I could go and wouldn't run out of room as I flipped down the beam toward my dismount. At this point, I didn't really need the assurance. I knew every single centimeter of that beam. But it was like a superstition: before I got on the beam, I always measured out an arm's length from one end and made a chalk mark to tell myself where my punch front should start, and before I dismounted I always touched the end of the beam with one foot.

Mo was waiting, arms crossed over her chest. I took a deep breath, feeling the area between my ribcage hollow and expand. I could do this. I *would* do this, not for National Championships or for Mo but for myself.

I launched into my round-off, and from the moment my hands touched the beam, I knew this time would be the same as all the others. My shoulders weren't angled toward the beam just right, and so I wasn't able to get the push I needed, which slowed everything else down. Because I didn't have the power going into my round-off, I also didn't have the momentum in my back handspring, so my feet felt like lead as I opened up into my full-twisting double back.

I saw the mat coming toward me only a split second before my feet hit, but it felt like I wasn't done flipping. My body was propelled forward, and I reached out a hand to touch the ground, one knee dropping to the blue foam as I landed. In a competition, that would have been considered a fall, and would have cost me the hope of any medal at all, much less gold.

A cloud of chalk puffed into the air as I slammed my fist against the mat. Mo shook her head. "Focus," she said. "You are not yourself today."

I felt like I hadn't been myself in a long time. Even the other girls were giving me darting sidelong glances, as though they were waiting for me to start growing and bust out of my leotard like the Incredible Hulk. I looked over in Scott's direction, hoping that he hadn't been witness to my utter failure.

Scott was talking to Cheng, who was making some motion with his hands that seemed to indicate that Scott's body position should be straighter. Scott nodded, his eyes never leaving Cheng's. I was relieved he hadn't been watching me mess up, but I was also a little disappointed. I felt like I kept tabs on most of his movements, whereas he could go an entire day without glancing in my direction at all.

I wanted to catch his attention, and I'd had an idea the other night that might turn out to be a way to do it. "Mo," I said. "About my beam mount. I was wondering . . ."

She looked at me expectantly. I took a deep breath. I'd never really tried to personalize my routine before. I always figured that Mo and Cheng were the experts, and so I would just do whatever they told me.

"I was watching a routine of my mom's on the internet," I said, "and she used to do this really cool mount. It was like a Silivas, only she rotated more times and . . ."

Mo nodded. "I've seen," she said. "She would get it named for her if she do at world competition, but she did not have chance."

The Silivas mount was named after a superfamous Romanian gymnast from the 1980s. Instead of my current boring beam mount, I would jump on a springboard and into a neckstand on the beam (like a headstand except that my head would be in front of the beam, my arms gripping it from behind). I would straddle my legs, then make them straight again as I turned to face the other way, then straddle again, then back to straight as I turned one more time. When my mom had done it, it had looked cool and interesting and beautiful.

"So, do you think I could change my mount?" I asked.

This new mount looked deceptively simple, but I knew that it would be a challenge to learn. For one thing, it would put pressure on my shoulders, and would require a ton of upper-body strength.

Mo considered this idea for a moment, as though she had had the same thought and was gauging whether or not I could do it. I was already working on a new dismount, so I knew this was a lot to take on.

"We could work on it," Mo said. "Now, practice almost over, so we will start tomorrow."

I glanced at Scott again, but he was still working with Cheng over by the rings and didn't look in my direction at all. He would, though, once I showed off my new mount. And my mom would be so proud of me. I couldn't wait.

Mo called us all to attention before we rotated to our next apparatus. "News crew is coming to talk to you," she announced.

There was an eruption of excited whispering from Christina, Jessie, and Britt. I didn't say a word. I was already scared to death of any kind of public speaking, and now was the worst possible time to be asked to do this. I was having a hard enough time saying things to my family and friends, much less a stranger or 20,000 viewers at home.

"Settle down," Mo said. "This reporter wants to ask you questions about the National Championships. You be polite, humble, answer a few questions, and then get to work on your tumbling passes with Cheng. She will tape that, too. Understand?"

"Do we have time to touch up our makeup?" Christina asked. I shot her a quick glance. I hadn't even known she wore makeup to practice, although I guess there was no way she could have been born with eyelashes that long and perfectly separated.

Mo didn't dignify Christina's question with a response, but the tightening of her mouth answered it well enough. "I introduce you to reporter, and you have ten minutes. Okay? Let's go."

It wasn't the same woman who'd interviewed

Scott a few weeks before. This woman wore a teal suit and had dyed-blond hair that looked as dry as tumbleweeds. With all that hair spray, it'd probably have ignited if you held a match next to it. I'd never seen her on TV, but I saw from the sticker on her microphone that she was from a rival news station to the one my parents usually watched. They didn't like the weatherman on her station, who'd once treated an incoming hurricane like it was a monster-truck event instead of a serious catastrophe.

"She's from my dad's station!" Jessie hissed to us as we approached. "But why would she want to talk to me? I'm not even technically an Elite yet."

Apparently, Mo was listening, because she gave Jessie a sharp look. "You are part of this team," she said. "You can be part of this, too."

The woman gave us a huge, red-lipstick smile. "Hi, y'all," she said in the heaviest Texas drawl I'd ever heard. I bet it was fake. "Y'all must be the talented girls I've been hearing all about. Sorry to interrupt your practice like this, but I just wanted to ask a few questions."

"Girls, this is Lyla Quin, from Channel Thirteen," Mo said. "Ms. Quin, you know the girls, yes?"

How did she know us? Had she been watching

us, or was she familiar with our gymnastics? The idea that I might actually have been on someone's radar as a gymnast to watch was kind of exciting, even if it added a bit of pressure.

"Please," Lyla said, "is there a place I can do the interviews?"

Mo led us into the pit room, where we usually went to practice our big skills into a huge pit filled with foam. Lyla fussed at her cameraman for a few minutes, directing him to move various equipment to get the best shot possible. In the end, she had us sit on top of a tall stack of mats, lined up in front of a huge banner that advertised an invitational event that had been held at Texas Twisters a couple of years ago.

I tried surreptitiously to smooth my hair, wishing I had a mirror so I could check to see if I had any flyaways. Considering that I *always* had a halo around my head of tiny baby hairs that escaped from my ponytail, I'm sure I did.

But Lyla Quin was a professional. She handed Christina a tissue to blot her face, saying it was shiny (Christina's smile slipped a little bit at that), told Britt to sit up straighter, and tapped me, telling me to cross my legs at the ankles instead of at the knees. Then she spent a minute talking to the cameraman in weird code about wide-angle shots and making sure everything was "in frame," before sliding her tongue over her teeth and turning to face the camera.

"Ready?" she asked, but it was more like a statement than a question, because she didn't wait for anyone to respond. The cameraman counted down from three, and Lyla started talking.

"We're here with four very talented young ladies," she said in that twang, "who are on their way to gymnastics greatness at the Junior National Championships coming up in Philadelphia. They took time from their very busy schedules to chat with us and tell us what it's like to follow your dreams."

And then, suddenly, the microphone was on me. I felt like a deer in the headlights, and I only hoped I didn't look like one.

"Noelle, you already qualified for the competition through a training camp earlier this year. What was that experience like?"

Didn't they tell you the questions they were going to ask before they put you on the spot? Or was that only for when Drew Barrymore went on Letterman or something? "Um," I said, "it was great."

Lyla Quin's smile got wider, but I swear she was thinking, What an idiot. How could she not? *It was great?* Christina said it was best to be vague, but this had to be taking it too far.

"It's a relief," I added, trying to think of something more interesting to say, "knowing I definitely have a spot."

Did that fit in with what Christina had said about not appearing too arrogant, but also not seeming like you were unsure of yourself? What did it matter? It was true that I'd had a perfect opportunity after the training camp, but it was also true that I'd completely blown it by now.

Lyla Quin moved on to Jessie then, asking about when she was going to qualify for the Elite team. I had to hand it to this woman; she'd done her homework. Jessie stumbled through her answer; I could tell she was thinking of what Christina had said, too, and trying to remember what the ideal answer was supposed to be.

Then Christina fielded a question about how long she'd been doing gymnastics (since she was five), and finally, Lyla Quin asked Britt what it was like to be homeschooled. She must have really gotten some background on each of us from Mo.

It made me a little nervous about what she'd ask me next.

"Actually, it sucks," Britt said. "I get left out of everything. And it's not even like I have less homework, because my grandmother is like a Nazi about education."

I saw Christina roll her eyes. It was obvious that Britt hadn't listened to any of her advice, but then, Britt marched to her own beat. I tensed up as Lyla Quin pushed the microphone into my face again.

"Gymnastics is mostly an individual sport," she said. "How do you balance that with being on a team like Texas Twisters?"

"Oh," I said, and then I meant to follow it up with something, but my mind went blank. There were times when gymnastics did feel very isolating; even when you were competing on a team, it was always just you up there on that apparatus, hoping to land your skills and stick your dismount. Mostly, I really loved having other girls to talk to, friends who were going through the same stuff that I was going through and could relate. But lately, I wasn't feeling so connected. It kind of seemed like I was up on that beam alone, struggling to keep my balance, but no one was spotting me.

Christina broke in, giving a flip of her hair that seemed practiced. Because it totally was—I remembered her doing it during Britt's fake interview of her on the Ferris wheel. "Being a gymnast might be like walking a tightrope, but your teammates are your net. So of course we love being part of a team."

I frowned. That made it sound like Christina was the main gymnast, and we were all just there to support *her*. I mean, who wanted to be the net when you could be the acrobat? I wondered if that was another technique her publicity coach had made her practice—Christina could still be arrogant, but she seemed to be getting better at making it more subtle.

Lyla Quin asked us a few more questions before gesturing to the cameraman to stop rolling tape. He lowered the camera from his shoulder—it looked heavy—and Lyla Quin fluffed her already gigantic hair.

"Thanks, y'all!" Her voice dripped with syrupy sweetness. "That was fabulous. Now, Pete and I are going to get some footage of y'all training, okay? Don't be self-conscious around the camera; just pretend it's not there and do what you do."

I had already probably made a fool of myself in the interview. Knowing my luck, I'd mess up on floor, too. It was a good thing Lyla Quin hadn't gotten any footage of beam practice. I started to head out of the pit room back to the main area, but the other girls were hanging back. I paused in the doorway to listen.

"You can cut out the part where I called my grandmother a Nazi, right?" Britt was saying. "I didn't mean she was actually a *fascist*, you know, I was just trying to say that she really gets on me about my homework."

"Did my face still look shiny on camera?" Christina asked. "If you give me a few minutes, I could touch up and give you another interview. We could talk about whatever you wanted. I bet a lot of your viewers don't know what a day in the life of a gymnast is like."

It was actually quite tedious. Training, school, training, and then home to sleep. Don't get me wrong, I usually felt most myself in the gym, but to an outsider it was probably just as interesting as watching a golf game on TV was for me.

Lyla Quin did a good job of deflecting all the questions, but she stopped to consider Jessie's, which was about Jessie's dad.

"Mark Ivy," Jessie said. "He's one of the anchors on your channel. Do you know him?"

It seemed like a strange thing to ask. Of course Lyla Quin knew Mark Ivy. They worked for the same station.

But from the sudden downturn of the corners of Lyla Quin's mouth, it seemed that maybe Mr. Ivy wasn't well liked at the station. She hid her feelings quickly behind her toothpaste smile; I wondered if Jessie even saw it.

"Oh, Mark," she gushed. "Right, yes. He's such a dynamic anchor. He really has a presence."

"He's going to take me camping soon," Jessie said. "Since I'm not going to Nationals. He was supposed to take me over Christmas break, but it didn't work out."

"Well, great," Lyla Quin said. "That's just great, sweetie. Now, I promised your coach I'd have you back at practice soon, so let's get on out there, and we can get the rest of our footage and be out of your hair."

At this, the other girls reluctantly made their way toward the door, but this time it was I who hung back to talk to Lyla Quin.

"Uh, Ms. Quin?" It was weird to call her that, but I didn't feel comfortable calling an adult by her first name. On television, she was always Lyla

Quin, but it also felt weird to use her full name in person.

"Yes, honey?" She pushed some of her hair-sprayed bangs out of her eyes.

"What made you come here today?" I asked. "I mean, why did you do these interviews?"

She chuckled, but it was a kind laugh. "I heard that four of our country's best gymnasts were right here in Austin, Texas," she said, "and that the competition of their lives was just around the corner. Now, that's too good a story to pass up."

And then she leaned in closer, so only I could hear. "And you know what? I was told that there was a little powerhouse named Noelle Onesti, and that she was the one to keep my eye on. So I'll be watching you, little girl. Do Austin proud."

Somehow I managed a weak smile. At this point, I couldn't imagine making anyone proud, much less the entire state capital.

When I arrived at the store that evening, covered in a sheen of sweat from the workout and the bike ride home in the Texas summer heat, Tata was behind the counter. The rush was over, and he had the television muted behind him as he usually did when things were slow. I saw that it was tuned to News Channel 8, and I was glad that my parents hated that weatherman on Channel 13, although I was curious to see the feature myself. In other circumstances, I would have been totally excited for my parents to see it. They'd have wanted to tape it and send copies to my relatives in Romania. Or Mama would bug Radu to help her figure out "that YouTube thing" until she could post it.

"Hi, Tata," I said, sliding onto a stool next to him.

"How was gym?" he asked, just like he always did.

Usually, I tried to find the best, most exciting thing to tell my father—whether I'd learned a new skill or gotten praise for my execution or finally mastered a difficult dance move. But the only good part had been getting the go-ahead to work on Mama's old beam mount, and something told me to keep that a secret for now. Plus, I felt drained of energy, and it was difficult to muster excitement about much of anything. My conversation with Lyla had reminded me of how serious my family's situation was right now.

"Hard," I said. "And tiring. I can't seem to get my new beam dismount."

"You'll get it," he said.

I leaned my elbows on the counter, resting my chin in my hands. "I don't know," I said. "I might not. Everyone has a limit to their abilities, I guess."

"What is this dismount?"

Even though my father wasn't as knowledgeable about gymnastics as my mother was, he still knew some of the lingo. It was impossible not to pick it up after living with me and Mama.

"It's the same as my old one, a tucked double back, but now I'm adding a full twist to the first flip. I can't seem to get enough height to complete all the rotations without messing up the landing."

"You will," he said. "You need to believe in yourself."

Of course, that was what a parent would say, and I appreciated it. But it also wasn't that easy. "It's like, if you told me I could fly if I believed hard enough, that doesn't mean that I actually would. I could jump off the top of a building and believe all I wanted, and I'd fall flat on my face."

Tata looked at me then, his brown eyes serious. I'd never realized how much Mihai looked like my dad, but they had the same eyes, deep-set, with the ability to level you in an instant.

"When you're in that gym, what do you think you are doing?" he said. "You are defying gravity. You are doing things that most people would call impossible. And do you know how you do it?"

"How?"

"Faith," he said. "Faith makes you fly."

Twelve

Christina and Britt left at the end of the month for the U.S. Classic, and Mo went with them. I wished them the best of luck, and I meant it—I really hoped that someone from our gym would be able to go to the National Championships, and they deserved it.

There were sixteen spots open, which meant that the top fourteen girls at the U.S. Classic would go on to compete at Nationals. Christina and Britt could nab two of those spots easily. Christina's routines weren't as difficult as Britt's, but she had the artistry and elegance that Britt sometimes forgot about in her quest to pull off the biggest tricks.

At one point, I thought I had the complete package. Ballet training from when I was younger made me more conscious of my body's movements and helped me with the required dance elements, and I tried to be meticulous about all of the little details. I wasn't as fearless as Britt, as muscular as Jessie, or as graceful as Christina, but I worked hard.

Maybe that was just what Christina's ridiculous publicity coach was always telling her, about how you were setting yourself up for failure if you were too arrogant. I'd focused so much on making my gymnastics perfect and believed so deeply that I really was one of the best that I'd been blind to other things. Like how hard it was to think about medals when everything else was falling apart.

The U.S. Classic wasn't being broadcast on television, but I'd promised Britt and Christina that I would watch the streaming webcast of it online. Since Jessie wasn't at the Classic, either, because she was preparing for her Elite qualifier coming up, she invited me over to her house to watch it. It would definitely beat trying to convince Radu to get off his World of Warcraft game and let me use the computer for a couple of hours, and then trying to listen to the commentary through only one speaker, while the twins screamed in the background. I agreed right away.

So that was how I found myself with a Saturday off for a change—or at least a half day, since we had trained with Cheng that morning. But by that afternoon, we were at Jessie's house, setting out chips and dip in the kitchen in anticipation of the webcast's starting. Jessie's stepdad had even figured out a way to use the Wii to show it on their big-screen TV.

"There's no way we're going to be able to eat all of these," I said, lining up the bags of salt-and-vinegar; sour-cream-and-onion; cheddar cheese; regular; and ridged chips, not to mention the pretzels and tortilla chips with salsa.

"I know," Jessie said. "But when my mom found out I was having friends over, much less for a party with *food*, she went a little nuts. My stepbrother and stepsister will polish off what we don't eat, believe me."

The first thing I focused on was Jessie's emphasis on the word *food*, which reminded me that she was still going through treatment for her eating disorder, even though none of us ever talked about it. I hoped she hadn't thought I was being insensitive in my comment. It was easy to think that she was all better now, but of course I knew that it wasn't that simple.

But then I realized that she'd used the plural, and I had to ask. "Friends?" I said. "Who else are you expecting?"

She gave me a sheepish look. "I kind of told some other people from the gym that they could come over and watch the competition at my house." Just then, the doorbell rang, and she brightened. "That could be them now."

"Wait, who?"

We heard the heavy footsteps of Jessie's step-brother pounding down the stairs as he raced to get the front door, and Jessie sprinted to get there first. "I've got it!" she yelled up. Then, to me, she said, "Felicia, Carolina, Jacob, and Scott."

She was opening the door and greeting her new guests, but I was reeling. *Scott?* She'd invited Scott over? I glanced down at myself. I was wearing a stretched-out old T-shirt from a competition I'd gone to five years ago and my cutoff jean shorts that I wore when I was just hanging out. They were house clothes, or spending-the-day-with-a-close-friend-who-doesn't-care clothes. They were *not* crush clothes.

But Scott was coming through the door, smiling at something Jacob was saying. His eyes flickered over me for a moment while he said hello, and then he was making his way toward the chips in the kitchen, arguing with Jacob about whether salt-and-vinegar chips were gross or delicious. (I said "delicious," but Scott seemed to think they were disgusting. I made a mental note not to touch the salt-and-vinegar chips.)

Felicia and Carolina followed the boys in, but I barely paid them any attention as I tried to decide on the coolest way to approach Scott. Maybe, I thought, I should ask him if his ankle was feeling better—I'd seen him roll it in practice a few days ago, but he seemed to be putting his full weight on it again. Then again, I didn't want to come off as a stalker.

I reached for a handful of pretzels at the same time as Scott did, figuring that our hands would brush against each other and it would be the perfect opportunity to strike up a conversation.

He drew his hand back. "Sorry," he said. "You look like a girl on a mission for pretzels."

Great. Now he thought I was some rude pig who'd practically shoved him out of the way for a stupid snack. I compensated by taking a single pretzel. "I just, um, wanted to try one," I said. Then I added, "I've never had a pretzel before."

Scott knitted his brows together. "Really?" he said. "I didn't think there was anyone on the planet who'd never had a pretzel. They're awesome."

I was going to ask him why he wasn't at the U.S. Classic, even though I knew that the men's qualifier didn't happen at the Classic, but then Jessie called into the kitchen, "Come on, guys, it's on!"

We all filed into the living room. I tried to stay a step behind Scott so I could find a seat next to him, but he chose an armchair, leaving me standing stupidly in the middle of the room while the girls piled onto the couch and Jacob sat cross-legged on the floor.

Jessie moved over a fraction of an inch. "There's room for you, Noelle," she said. "Sometimes our stunted growth pays off, right?"

Everyone shifted, but I still had to squeeze myself between Jessie and the arm of the couch. It was not very comfortable.

"Look!" Felicia said, pointing at the screen. Felicia was fourteen, but only a Level Seven gymnast. I'd always felt kind of weird around gymnasts who were close to my age but at a lower level. It wasn't that I was trying to be snobbish or cliqueish . . . but when you trained six days a week for up to eight hours a day with the same three people, it was easy to pretend that the other gymnasts didn't exist. I was surprised Jessie had invited them at all, even though I knew it was the nice thing to do.

The picture on the TV was a little pixilated—a full-screen webcast through a Wii on a big-screen television did have some limitations, after all—but we could see a list of the competing athletes' names scrolling down. On that list, in big letters, it said: CHRISTINA FLORES, and then, BRITTANY MORGAN. We let out a little cheer.

We watched a few routines from other gymnasts, including an almost flawless bars set from Peyton Clarke, who was probably one of my biggest rivals (not personally—I'd barely spoken to her—but on the gymnastics floor). She was really good, and the only reason she hadn't been chosen at the training camp was because she'd had tendinitis in her elbow and had been forced to sit it out. But now she was back, healthy again and apparently better than ever. I knew she'd be a threat at Nationals. I'd have loved to challenge her right then and there, but I had to settle for the hope the other girls could do the job for me.

And then Britt was up on the balance beam. It was strange to see her on TV, her blond hair back in her usual ponytail, that familiar steely look in her eye as she waited for the signal to mount the apparatus. And yet there was something slightly different about her. . . .

"Oh, my god," I said. "Is Britt wearing *makeup*?"

Jessie laughed. "It's a competition, Noelle. You know you have to wear it to look good for the judges. Otherwise, all they see out there is your pasty, washed-out face."

I did, in fact, know that. Maybe it was because Britt was such a tomboy and this was the first time I'd actually seen her at a competition, but for some reason the sight of her face all covered in foundation and her lips unnaturally glossy totally threw me for a loop.

"Even Scott wears makeup for big meets," Jacob said. Scott made a fist, pretending he was about to throw a punch. The men's gymnastics program wasn't very big at Texas Twisters, and at sixteen, Jacob was the oldest boy in the class, which consisted of seven-year-olds on up. It must have been frustrating to have to practice with all different levels, but we didn't have the equipment or the resources to field competitive teams at each age level. Scott was eighteen, and technically not part of the Texas Twisters team. He received some private training from Cheng, and then, once the fall semester started, he'd be at Conner University with the collegiate team.

I turned back to the television just in time to see Britt mount the beam with her powerful punch-front move. She launched into her first acrobatic series right off the bat, but when she landed her back layout, one of her feet shot out from underneath her. Her leg went up and she bent at the waist, but she managed to regain her balance and avoid the fall.

Still, it was not a good start.

I bit my lip. "Come on, Britt," I whispered.

Britt managed to finish her routine with no other major incident, but her face showed her frustration. I saw Mo put her arm around her shoulders and talk to her in that calm way she had. I could just hear what she'd be saying: *Don't worry about it; there are other events.*

"She'll be fine," Jessie said. "She only needs to make top fourteen here. She'll do it."

Christina started on vault, which was her least favorite event, but at least it meant that she got to end on floor, which was her specialty. She executed a clean Yurchenko with a full twist, but the relatively low level of difficulty meant that her score was only enough to put her in tenth place.

Scott clapped his hands. "It's okay, she'll get it."

I didn't know what would have been better: being there with Scott, or being cheered on by Scott. Even though I knew he'd root for any gymnast from Texas Twisters, there'd have been something so romantic about him watching *my* routines and wanting me to do well.

They didn't show Britt on floor, which was a shame, because she ended her routine with an awesomely high double back into a punch front. They did post her score, however, which I happened to know was a personal best for her. With that number, Britt moved into seventh place. She'd have been higher if not for that mishap on the beam, but at that point it didn't matter. Obviously, you always wanted to win a medal, but the most important thing at this competition was breaking the top fourteen.

Christina's routine on the uneven bars shifted her into sixth place, and then Britt executed two phenomenal vaults to move into fourth. They didn't show Christina's beam routine, even though that was always one of her best events, and today was no different. She posted a score high enough to move into fifth place, just behind Britt. It was proof that, in the current scoring system, big gymnastics often paid off more than stunning artistry. Christina had the long lines and grace, but her difficulty level was low compared to Britt's, so she trailed her, even though Britt had had a mistake on her first routine.

They didn't show Britt's uneven bars routine, either, but it must've been relatively clean, because it was enough to keep her steady at fourth place, but not amazing enough to advance her any higher. Still, fourth place meant that Britt was definitely going to the Junior Nationals, and we all shouted and high-fived each other.

It came down to Christina on the floor, but we weren't worried. Unless she had a disastrously awful routine, there was no way she'd miss making the cut. And although she ended up stepping out of bounds on her first pass, a tucked full-in that was relatively new for her, she easily scored high enough to keep herself in the running, even though she did drop one place in the standings.

The entire webcast took two hours; by the end of it, I felt as drained as if I'd actually competed. I also felt . . . depressed. Watching Christina and Britt out there, getting guidance from Mo and smiling as they saluted the judges, hearing the cheers from the crowd when the girls landed big skills, all made me ache to go to Junior Nationals. I wanted it so badly I almost didn't care anymore about my parents, or about the store, or about how much debt they'd have had to go into to send me. At that moment, I just wanted to compete in Philadelphia, more than anything else in the whole world.

"Well, thanks, Jessie," Scott was saying, picking up his paper plate from the coffee table. A boy who wasn't a complete slob like my brothers! I fell for him all over again. I wondered if I would ever work up the courage to talk to him.

"Thanks, Mrs. Ivy," Scott said to Jessie's mom, who was wiping down the kitchen counter.

Even though I knew that wasn't her name—Jessie's last name was Ivy, but her mom had remarried—she didn't correct Scott. "No problem," she said.

"My laptop is a million years old," Scott said. "I doubt it would've been able to stream this. Watching it on the big screen was pretty cool."

He and Jacob were walking toward the front door, as though they were already leaving. "Are you going to get a new laptop before college?" Jacob was asking. "I've heard that they're just a little important when you have all those term papers or whatever else to write."

And I remembered why it was so hard to talk to Scott: we were in completely different worlds. He was in the world of frat parties and late-night cram sessions, and I was still such a kid. He had goals and was working toward them—going to Nationals, then to college. I didn't know what I was working toward anymore, but at least I didn't feel as powerless as I had just a few weeks ago. I might not have been brave enough yet to talk to Scott, but I was sure that would change soon, too.

Thirteen

It seemed like I'd experienced this moment a thousand times over, every single night as I lay in bed and tried to visualize landing my full-twisting double-back dismount on beam. But nothing prepared me for how good it felt to actually do it, to feel the beam beneath my feet as I pushed off and launched myself high above the mat, my body already twisting, until I landed with my feet firmly planted. I didn't have to windmill my arms at all to keep my balance. I drilled it.

I was smiling so wide that I almost didn't hear Mo's praise. Landing it once in practice didn't mean that I'd nail it like that every time, but from now on it was all about muscle memory. My body had done it once, and so my body could be trained to do it again and again.

On top of that, I was really starting to get my new mount, and I couldn't wait to unveil it. Nationals would've been the perfect place, but now . . . Well, I guessed I would have to see what happened.

Christina and Britt had gotten back from the U.S. Classic all aglow from their competition experiences and pumped up for the Nationals. At that point, I'd completely resigned myself to the fact that I wasn't going. There would be other competitions, other opportunities. There was no point in dwelling on this one.

The deadline to register for a hotel room with the block reserved for our team had already passed, so there was no way around it. My only fear was admitting to Mo that I wasn't competing. She'd been so focused on getting Britt and Christina through the Classic that she hadn't paid as much attention to me, but I knew she thought it was a foregone conclusion that I'd be there representing the gym. I hated to let her down.

My plan had been to to approach Mo after practice, but on my way out of the locker room I spotted Mihai across the floor. He was talking to Christina, waving his arms and gesturing. I headed over to join them, wondering what he could possibly have to say to Christina. It had better not be anything embarrassing about me, like a story about the time he caught me dancing around my bedroom to "I Ran" by Flock of Seagulls. Tata had gotten really into some eighties music when he first came to this country, and sometimes I listened to his old CDs.

Mihai stopped talking when he saw me coming. This seemed very suspicious. I glanced from his face to Christina's, trying to figure out what was going on. "Hey," I said. "What are you doing here?"

Mihai shrugged. "Haven't you heard? Mama and Tata basically put me under house arrest. They're really serious about me not going anywhere but summer school and working at the store. The only way I could get them to let me out of the house was if I promised to ride my bike over here so you'd have some company on the ride home."

"Okay, but I have to talk to Mo first."

For some reason, that made Mihai dart a quick look at Christina. I studied both of them again. Christina had been my friend for a while, but she didn't come over a lot. If we were going to hang out outside of gym, we mostly met up at the mall, or sometimes I would go to her house, where they had cable. So it wasn't like Mihai and Christina had had a lot of opportunity to notice each other. From the phone calls I'd had to field at the house, I knew girls inexplicably seemed to think my brother was cute, and Christina had batted her eyelashes at him a couple of times, although I'd thought she was just being silly. I hoped that wasn't what this was about, because if Christina and my brother liked each other . . . Gross.

"I don't think we have time for that," Mihai said. "If I don't get you home in the next fifteen minutes, Mama's going to think I ran away and send out a search party."

"It's kind of important—" I said, but Christina cut me off.

"I need to talk to Mo, too," she said, "and I was here first."

I was a little taken aback. Hadn't she just been wasting time talking to my brother? Obviously her issue couldn't be *that* important. But when I pointed this out, she waved her hand.

"It's something to do with the Classic," she said. "You understand."

So, basically, because I hadn't competed, I was somehow less important. It was a nice preview of how things would be after the Nationals.

"Come on, Noelle," Mihai said. "Let's get going."

Once outside, Mihai and I unchained our bikes and headed for home. He signaled to me that he wanted to race, and suddenly it was like we were both five years younger, sailing down the streets at breakneck speed, weaving expertly around fire hydrants and other obstacles until we coasted onto the busier street where the store was located. That had always been our unspoken finish line, and as usual, Mihai broke it first.

"You'd think with that workout you do, you'd beat me for once."

"You have longer legs than I do," I pointed out. "And your bike is bigger. You have an unfair advantage."

Mihai laughed as we dumped our bikes in the storage shed behind the store. "Do your coaches listen to those excuses?"

No, they didn't. And I wasn't the type to make excuses, either, even when I had a legitimate one. One time I'd competed through an entire meet with a broken finger, because I didn't want Mo to think I was weak. After the competition, when she saw how purple and swollen my finger was, she told me I should've said something if I was in pain. But when you're a gymnast, some pain is acceptable. It's expected, even. So I'd fought through it.

Now, in this situation with Junior Nationals, I wondered if my parents would feel the same way. They'd been shelling out money for my gymnastics for years. There were the general expenses, like the monthly fees for my training, the equipment, and new leotards. We got some secondhand from other girls in the gym, but there were still times when I needed a new one for a competition. And then there were all the hidden expenses that you might not think about: the Ace bandages, heating pads, ice packs, medical visits, makeup and hair accessories for meets, and gas for travel.

Maybe, to my parents, needing to shell out thousands of dollars for one competition was the equivalent of competing with a broken finger. Sure, it hurt. But it was something you had to deal with, something you just had to find a way to get through, because you knew quitting wasn't an option.

When I rationalized it that way, I wanted to

race through the back door of that store and grab my father and let him make everything right. But the difference was that this time, it wasn't me with the broken finger. It was my parents, and instead of just a finger, it was like their whole hand was hurt. The entire body of our family was breaking down.

"I've really messed things up, haven't I?"

Mihai paused at the door to the storage shed. He'd been fastening the padlock, which we always kept locked even though most of what was in there was just old yard equipment and our bikes.

"Nah," he said. "Nothing that can't be fixed, anyway."

I kicked at the dirt, watching it speckle the toe of my sneaker. "Today was the deadline to register for the hotel," I said. "Which I obviously missed. And I know Mo submitted my name as one of her athletes competing. People are going to be asking where I am, and she's going to have to make excuses for me."

As Mihai had so accurately pointed out, Mo hated excuses, whether she was listening to them or making them herself. She said that excuses were the enemy of the truth.

"Don't worry about it," Mihai said. "It'll all work out."

Of course, Mihai could be nonchalant about everything. That was the way he'd always been. Even now, when he was in more trouble with our parents than ever before, he was still acting like it was no big deal.

"What about you?" I asked. "Did Mama and Tata find out about your job?"

He shot me a sharp look. "No—and I plan to keep it that way. Look, the carnival is only in town for another two weeks. I really need this, so don't blow it, okay?"

I'd never broken a promise in my life, so I was irritated that Mihai would doubt me now. "I said I wouldn't tell, and I won't. But don't you think that it would be better for them to know you're blowing off the store for another job than to think you're just doing it to hang out with your friends?"

"Are you going to tell them about Junior Nationals?"

Why did Mihai always make this comparison? My not telling our parents about the competition was to protect them, especially given all that was happening with the store and our house. The competition just wasn't going to happen, so there was no point in dwelling on it. Mihai's not telling about his job was . . . I didn't know.

I sighed. "You know I'm not," I said. "Anyway, it's too late now."

"Then don't worry about me." Mihai turned to face me as we reached the back entrance of the store, grabbing the handle and pushing against the door with his hip to open it.

"Trust me," he said.

And I did. I had no choice. Throughout my life, whenever there'd been times I felt like I couldn't trust myself, it had always been Mihai I'd put my trust in instead.

During the summer, we got an hour break for lunch in the middle of our training days. Sometimes, I biked home to eat a fresh sandwich from the store and hang out with Tata, but most days, I brought something to the gym and ate it there. At first, the other girls had teased me about my "weird" food, but they'd stopped once they tried some. No one could resist Mama's cooking.

Today, Mama had sent me to gym with a traditional Romanian casserole, Musaca de vinete, in the basket on the front of my bike. I knew that she could tell there was something going on with me, since she usually cooked big meals only for family occasions. Between our family and the store, she already had enough food preparation to worry about. But this morning, she'd wrapped clear cellophane tightly over the top and helped me load it onto my bike, telling me to share it with the other girls and to be sure to tell Mrs. Flores that she said hi.

So, when I saw Britt, Jessie, and Christina already sitting together in the concession area of the gym, I approached their table with the casserole, hoping to catch them before they'd already dug in to their own food. They were leaning over a notebook, where Christina was jotting down notes in between gesturing with her hands. As I came closer, Jessie said something to Christina out of the corner of her mouth, and the notebook disappeared.

"Hey, guys," I said, glancing at Britt, who'd moved the notebook to her lap. "What's up?"

"Nothing," Jessie said, while Britt said, "Oh, the usual."

My eyes darted among the three of them, trying to figure out why they were acting so strangely. "Okay . . . Well, my mother made Musaca de vinete, and I was wondering if you would want to share it." Self-doubt made my voice rise on the last few syllables.

"That sounds awesome," Britt said.

Christina shook her head. "We can't."

"It's mostly vegetables," I said. "And low-fat cheese. So, it's healthy."

"Sorry, Noelle," Jessie said. "We're just, um, kind of busy. Sorry."

The fact that she apologized twice made me very suspicious, along with the fact that I couldn't think of anything that the three of them would need to discuss or do without me. It couldn't be a high school thing, because Britt was there, and she was homeschooled and only going into the eighth grade. It couldn't be a U.S. Classic or Nationals thing, because Jessie was there, and she hadn't qualified for Elite competition yet. My birthday was on Christmas, so it couldn't be planning a surprise party or anything like that.

"Actually, we were just leaving," Christina said. "But your food looks yummy—you should totally enjoy it. We'll see you later, okay?"

Why would I want to eat lunch all by myself? But I just watched as they packed up their stuff, including the mysterious notebook, and I pretended I was totally cool with sitting alone, this giant casserole in front of me as a glaring reminder of my loser status.

I watched them leave, feeling rejected and dejected and depressed. A month ago, I'd been part of a team. I'd had friends who shopped for dresses together. Now, it seemed like I had nothing.

Using one of the plastic sporks I'd grabbed from the concession stand, I dug into the casserole, not bothering to cut off a slice. What was the point? I'd eat a little bit of it, then throw the rest away. I hated to be wasteful, but I wasn't going to let my mother know that my friends had abandoned me.

"Mind if I join you?"

I almost choked when I saw Scott standing over me, gesturing toward an empty chair. I wanted to shout that *of course* it was okay, but my mouth was full, and I wasn't about to gross him out with a vision of my mashed-up food. So I tried to tell him with a closemouthed smile, while continuing to chew, that he was more than welcome to sit down.

He raised his eyebrows, and I finally swallowed my bite.

"Yes," I said, "I mean, no, I don't mind."

He smiled at me. "That looks good. What's in it?"

I listed some of the key ingredients, which led to a discussion of what chard was, exactly, and before I knew it, Scott had a plastic spork of his own and was attacking the opposite side of the casserole. For the moment, the other girls were forgotten; I couldn't believe my luck. Scott Pattison was sitting with *me*! He was eating my mother's casserole! It was practically like we were married.

"So," I said. "You leave tomorrow for your qualifier, right?"

Luckily, he didn't ask why I seemed to know so much. It was common for gymnasts to keep track of each other, so it wasn't completely bizarre for me to know his schedule. Now, if he knew that I could name every single skill he competed in at each event, to the point where I could probably calculate his difficulty levels myself, that might come off a little stalkerish.

"Yeah," he said. "God, I hope I make it. I'm not really worried, though. I've been practicing like crazy all year—first to get that scholarship, then to prepare for the college team, and now for Nationals."

Scott didn't even need Christina's publicity

coach. He obviously knew the art of being confident without appearing cocky. If you worked hard and you earned something, there was no reason not to own it. I realized that that was the position I would've been in had I actually been going to the competition. I'd worked really hard, and I would have expected myself to do well. I guess I didn't expect to give myself the chance.

"Hey." He jabbed at the air with his spork, as though just remembering something. "Didn't you say you had some questions for me about the big meet? 'Cause if you do, shoot. I know the men's competition is a little different, but I'll do what I can to help."

It might've been a good idea to prepare some questions for this situation earlier, considering that I had pestered him twice now to give me this guidance. But first of all, I knew I wasn't going to Nationals, and second of all, I'd never imagined Scott would actually take the time to talk to me.

"Do you have a girlfriend?" I blurted out instead. I could've died.

He blinked but recovered quickly. "Uh . . . no, I don't."

I was itching to ask about the dark-haired mystery girl at the carnival, but again: stalkerish.

I feared I was sprinting down the runway toward Scott's thinking I was totally psychotic, and I tried to think of how to tie this conversation back to gymnastics.

Luckily, Scott did it for me. "Is that what this is about?" he asked. "Do you like someone? Is it messing up your head before the competition?"

"There is someone," I admitted truthfully.

"Well, I can tell you: don't let that boy come between you and your training. This is an important time, and you can't get it back. Don't let a crush make you lose sight of that." He glanced around the gym, craning his neck to look at the group of guys hanging out in the corner by the still rings. "Is it someone here? Is it Jacob?"

I looked over just in time to see Jacob shove his fist underneath his armpit, pumping his arm to make a farting noise that had the other guys slapping their thighs and laughing. Gross. "No, it's not Jacob," I said, and then I took a deep breath. "But it is someone at this gym."

Scott nodded. "In that case, he should understand your commitment as a fellow athlete. It's fine to flirt a little, but you really don't have time to date, not with the biggest competition of your life coming up." As if I needed to be reminded of that. "Is he going to Nationals?"

"He hopes to," I said.

There was a flash of something in Scott's eyes that I couldn't bear to look at, so I stared down at my white fingers gripping the plastic cutlery. "I'm sure that whoever it is," he said slowly, "is very flattered. And I'm also sure that whoever it is cares about you a lot . . . but sees you more as a younger sister."

"Who said he was older?" I said, just to save face. I could feel mine burning up.

"Nobody," Scott admitted with a rueful smile. "You're an amazing athlete, Noelle Onesti, and a very special person. Good luck at Nationals . . . Not that you'll need it."

And then he was getting up and walking away, before I even had time to register the fact that he'd pronounced my last name correctly. My casserole was completely cold, but inside I felt even colder. I guess if I had been honest with myself, I'd always known that there was no way Scott would ever *really* be with me. If there was one thing I'd learned in the past couple of months, it was that there was a big difference between having a pipe dream and having no dream at all.

Fourteen

Usually, I almost dreaded our Sundays off from gym. Don't get me wrong—
the rest was welcome after a bone-crunching, muscle-straining, body-pounding week.
Once, I'd seen this thing on *60 Minutes* about a football player who was exempt from Monday and Tuesday workouts because he literally couldn't get out of bed after Sunday's game. They showed him covered with ice packs, and then they showed the way he dragged himself around his house, as though walking upright took every last breath. They showed footage of him on Sundays, running full speed into grown men each weighing two hundred and fifty

pounds, as though his only goal in life was to crush them.

Most weeks, I could relate. Sure, I was tired and I ached all over from my workouts, but it was all worth it for the adrenaline of sticking that dismount or nailing a release skill on bars. Being away from that environment made me feel somewhat empty. It was as though I was never as much myself as when I was in the gym, and every Monday I breathed in the familiar smell of chalk and sweat as though it were my first time.

But this Sunday, I found myself wishing I never had to go back. First, I had sabotaged my own gymnastics career. Then, my friends had completely deserted me, and although I wanted to play the victim and say I couldn't understand why, I thought I had a good idea. I just wasn't fun anymore. Ever since Mo had handed me that envelope, I'd become a neurotic mess, a tangle of nerves and anxieties that prevented me from enjoying hanging out, or enjoying the carnival or gymnastics. I couldn't blame them for not wanting to be around me—*I* didn't particularly want to be around me.

And then there was that mortifying incident with Scott.

I buried my face in my bedspread, as though the moment were replaying right there in my bedroom and I couldn't stand to see it. Although I'd been awake for hours, I'd been just lying there, my thoughts traveling a pessimistic circle from gymnastics to Scott to my family and my friends and back to gymnastics. And every time I got to the memory of the look on Scott's face when he realized that *he* was the guy I had a crush on . . .

I purposely shoved that from my mind. I had too much else to worry about for the upcoming week. Today, I got to relax, but tomorrow, I had a plan that could change my family's future.

There was a rap on my door before Mihai burst in.

"Don't you knock?"

"I did," he said, which was technically true, although common courtesy usually dictates waiting for a response before barging in. "Get up. Get dressed. There's something you have to see."

I had been looking forward to a day when I didn't change out of my white tank top and my blue shorts with the word TUMBLE across the butt. The plan was to stay in bed until noon, get up for food, bring my lunch back into my room, and then maybe take a postmeal nap until dinnertime or until the twins woke me up, whichever came first. My plan definitely did *not* include leaving the house.

I told Mihai that, but he just ripped the quilt off my bed, leaving me exposed to the cold air. Desperately, I tried to reach for the cover, but he dumped it on the floor.

"Come on," he said. "We're already late."

"Late for what?" I was still annoyed, but I realized I wasn't going to win this battle. Plus, I was actually starting to get a little curious.

"Don't worry about it," he said. "Just hurry up!"

With that, Mihai left, slamming the door behind him. I lay in bed for a few seconds, still debating trying to continue my plan of relaxation, but the window for that had already passed. It was like when you woke up and wanted to hold on to the last lingering remnants of a dream, but it was too late. So I scrambled up and stood in front of my closet, wondering what you wore to such a mysterious event.

In the end, I threw on a pair of shorts and a T-shirt. Mihai wasn't in the apartment; when I went downstairs, he wasn't in the store, either. The whole place was oddly quiet, and I wondered if Mama and Tata had taken the twins to the park or something.

Since the store was open only a half day on Sunday, they usually tried to do something fun like that, to make up for the amount of time the twins spent cooped up in that small apartment during the week.

I found Mihai outside, unchaining our bikes. "Are you going to tell me what this is all about?"

"Nope," he said without a moment's hesitation, and then he was off on his bike, trusting me to follow.

I wondered if Mama and Tata were okay with wherever he was taking me and whatever we were doing. The carnival had left town, which meant that he was back to hanging around the store a lot and sticking closer to home. It seemed to have mollified them a bit, but they still watched him warily, as though at any moment he might go back to sneaking out. For the time being, I guess they just breathed a sigh of relief to see him working at the store, his geometry textbook propped up on the counter for when it was slow and he could cram in some summer-school homework.

He was pedaling faster than I'd ever seen him, his feet like whirlwinds as he wended his way down the streets. Even though we hadn't officially announced a race, I was fighting to keep up, flying

216

toward a finish line I couldn't see. It wasn't until we came to a familiar intersection that I guessed our destination.

"The gym?" I asked while we waited for the light to let us cross. "Really? On a Sunday? Mihai, this is really the last place—"

"Trust me," he said, and I had only a second to reflect on the fact that he'd been asking me to do that a lot lately when we got the green light and were off again.

I rarely saw the gym on a Sunday. A few times, when I'd been in the lower levels, we'd had Sunday competitions and would all meet up in the parking lot to carpool to San Antonio or Houston or Fort Worth. Then, the parking lot had been mostly empty, except for a couple of parents' vans or SUVs, the coolers and other supplies spread out over the asphalt as everyone figured out the logistics of who was riding in what car.

Now, there were a ton of cars in the parking lot. They were lined up out into the street, and Mihai and I had to navigate a maze of large vehicles trying to wedge themselves into compact spaces. Finally, we reached the front door of the gym.

"What is this?" I asked. Across the lot, Christina, Jessie, and Britt were hard at work washing cars. It looked like they were having a fair amount of fun, too. As I watched, Britt took her sponge and demonstrated a "Wax On, Wax Off" move on one of the cars for Jessie, who pretended to karate-chop Britt's outstretched arm.

So this was what they'd been whispering about that day. They'd been planning this car wash, and for whatever reason, they hadn't wanted me to know. I didn't get it. I was a hard worker. I could have washed cars with the best of them. Even though I'd been a bit of a downer lately, I could still have fun. But they hadn't thought to include me.

Mihai hopped off his bike, letting it fall to the sidewalk, but I stayed seated on mine, with one foot on the ground for support. "Great," I muttered. "I don't know how you found out about this, but thanks for showing me. It's just what I needed."

He glanced at me, his brown eyes searching mine. "Don't you get it, Noelle? This is all for you."

And then I looked around me. I mean, *really* looked. I saw the hand-lettered signs: SEND NOELLE TO NATIONALS! I saw Christina directing cars, tearing sheets of paper from a yellow pad to make impromptu receipts. I saw Scott and Jacob and Felicia and others from the gym tackling cars with sudsy water and soft rags (Scott looked adorable in his wet T-shirt and swimming trunks, I couldn't help noticing). I saw Mo standing to one side, smiling in a way I never saw her do in practice. And then I turned around, and I saw my parents.

"I—" I started to say, but couldn't get the words out. This car wash was for *me*?

Mama hugged me fiercely, pressing my face into her shirt. "Why couldn't you tell us?" she asked. "You know we would've done anything to make sure you could follow your dream."

That was exactly what I'd been afraid of, but it all seemed so silly now. "I know," I said. "I'm sorry. . . . I just got tired of holding our family back just because of my dream."

Tata gave my shoulder an affectionate squeeze. "*Our* dream is to see you happy," he said. As always, he didn't have a lot of words, but he had the right ones.

"But the house—" I said. "There has to be a way to get some kind of extension, or break, or something."

"Actually," Mama said, her gaze darting to Tata, as though checking to make sure it was okay to share the news with me, "we've already spoken with the bank, and we were able to work something out."

"We're not going to lose the house? Or the store?"

Mama shook her head. "No," she said. "We're all going to have to live on an even tighter budget, but we can make it work. The bank has agreed to take lower payments for a couple of years, and hopefully the economy will get better in the meantime and things will pick up."

Mama gestured to a group of kids, including the twins, who were jumping through the water from a sprinkler in the grass next to the gym. Mrs. Morgan, Britt's mom, waved to us from where she was watching them.

"And Pam has offered to watch the twins part-time during the day at her daycare, so that will free up more time for me to work in the store," Mama said. "They seem to already love playing with some of her other kids."

"Wow," I said. "That offer might not last, once she sees how crazy they are. I'd use that extra time to go get your nails done or something."

Mostly, I needed to lighten up the situation before I totally broke down. I could feel the tightness in the back of my throat from the flood of emotions I was feeling just then—relief, gratitude, awe. My mother must have sensed it, because she gently pushed me toward the action.

"Go on," she said. "Get in there and get your hands dirty."

First I turned to Mihai. "This was you, wasn't it? You did this."

"Not exactly," he said. "I made you a promise I wouldn't tell Mama and Tata about Junior Nationals, and I didn't. But I did tell Christina, who put this car wash together to raise some money for you to go, and *she* told Mama, so technically, I didn't break my promise."

Mihai dug in his back pocket, pulling out a folded piece of paper. "Also, I went ahead and used my carnie money to buy you a round-trip ticket to Philadelphia. Good thing they gave me extra hours, or else it would've been one way."

I unfolded the paper. It was a confirmation e-mail from an airline, with my name listed as the passenger. I'd never flown on a plane for a competition before, and I couldn't believe I was going to get to now.

I enveloped Mihai in a huge hug, making him stagger back a bit. I could tell he was taken aback by my show of affection, but then he wrapped his arms around me, too.

"You're the best brother ever," I whispered.

He laughed. "You have three other brothers who might have something to say about that. Now, enough of this mushy stuff—you can't let everyone else do the dirty work for your own fund-raiser. Go wash some cars!"

It was almost noon, and the sun was high in the sky. Normally, I found the Texas summer heat oppressive, but today it seemed like the perfect weather to be outside in, hosing down cars and gulping down Gatorade. Jessie and Britt saw me coming toward them and smiled.

"Sorry," Jessie said. "I know we were acting kind of weird before. I hope you get that it was nothing personal. We were trying to keep this on the down low."

I picked up a sponge and wrung it out, adding more water to the puddles that were already gathering under a shiny red truck. "How could I be mad? This is totally awesome. If anything, I'm sorry. I haven't been the best friend lately. I guess I was distracted with all of this stuff."

"It's okay."

Maybe, but that didn't make it right. It occurred

to me that I wasn't the only person who had been going through some stuff this summer, though I'd been so caught up in my own drama that I really hadn't paid much attention to anyone else's.

"When do you leave for your camping trip?" I asked. I remembered that Jessie had been looking forward to the chance to see her dad. It couldn't have been the mosquitos or having to use leaves as toilet paper that had gotten her all excited. Personally, I didn't see the point in roughing it.

Jessie's eyes clouded over, and I immediately wished I could take the question back. "Oh . . . it didn't work out."

It was common knowledge that Jessie's dad flaked out on her a lot, so I wasn't going to bother with any follow-up questions, since I figured that was what had happened. But then Britt cut in, trying to prevent anything that might make Jessie feel worse.

"It's all good, right, Jess?" Britt flicked water from her wet fingers in my direction, and I made a show of wiping the droplets off my arm, although I was smiling. "Now you get to come to Junior Nationals instead and watch us totally rock everyone else off the beam."

Even though Britt was new at the gym, she'd

already become protective of Jessie. Meanwhile, I'd been friends with Christina for years, but rather than tell her what was going on with me, I had shut down and shut her out. And yet, she'd arranged all of this, because she knew I needed help.

I tried to catch Christina's gaze, but she was on the other side of the parking lot talking to a woman with big hair whom I didn't recognize. Then Britt nudged me, gesturing toward someone getting out of a dark blue hatchback.

"Hey," she said. "Isn't that David?"

He was scanning the parking lot, clearly looking for someone, and a couple of weeks earlier, I would've ducked out of sight. But now, for some reason, I felt my heart lift a little at seeing him. The sun was glinting off his glasses in a dorkier version of the classic slow-motion shot of an action star walking in the light, and he was wearing a *Star Wars* shirt and jeans with a hole in one knee.

"He might be here for an encore of his performance at the dance," Britt said, wiggling her eyebrows. "Want me to be bounce him? I could be, like, your security."

"No," I said absently. Whoever was driving the car he'd come in had pulled around to the line of cars waiting for a wash, and David was standing in the middle of it all now, his hands in his pockets. I handed my sponge to Britt without looking to see if she had a grip on it, accidentally soaking the front of her shirt more than it already was.

"Guess not," she said, but I was already walking off toward David. He finally spotted me and met me halfway.

"Hi," he said.

"Hi."

And then there was awkward silence for a moment, until I said, "Look, I'm sorry—"

"This is really—" he started to say at the same time; he laughed. "Go ahead."

"Okay." I took a deep breath. "I'm sorry I kind of blew you off before. It's just that I'm not used to this sort of thing, and—"

"And you don't like me that way," he finished for me. "It's okay, Noelle. I get it. You have a lot going on right now. I think you're really cool and smart and sweet, and I wanted to let you know that I'm willing to settle for being your friend. I saw on the news that your friends were doing this fund-raiser, and I thought, I want to be her friend, too. I want to do anything I can to help you get to Nationals."

This was a lot to process, but one thing he'd said especially stuck out, and I felt the need to address that first. "The news?" I said. "What are you talking about?"

"Channel Thirteen." Seeing my blank expression, he explained, "They advertised this car wash last night, telling people to come out and support a local gymnast. It was a follow-up to that interview you guys did. You were great in that, by the way."

I still hadn't had a chance to view that piece, although I knew that Jessie had recorded it on her DVR, and Britt had probably uploaded it to the internet already. I wasn't sure I ever wanted to see it. The idea of having to watch myself, hear my own voice, made me shudder.

Glancing over at Christina, I realized now who she was standing with. It was Lyla Quin, the reporter who'd done that interview with us. I wanted to go over there and thank them both for everything, but first there was something else I had to do.

Before I could second-guess myself (because if I'd waited even a second, I definitely would've chickened out), I stood on my tiptoes and gave David a quick kiss on the cheek.

He immediately turned as red as the Camaro

behind him, raising his a hand to the spot where my lips had been. "What was that for?" he said, a goofy smile on his face.

I didn't want to look over at Scott, in case David followed my gaze and got the wrong idea. But I could picture him—his perfect teeth, blue eyes, the way his hair curled a little bit at the nape of his neck if he hadn't had a haircut in a while. And I realized that that was all Scott had ever been to me—a picture in my head. It was beautiful, but it wasn't real. I knew all this trivia about Scott Pattison, like what ankle he'd sprained before and what movie he'd seen three times in the theater, but I didn't really know *him*.

I didn't know David, either, but I wanted to.

"I still can't do this right now," I said, which had to be the most awkward thing anyone could possibly say after kissing, but I hoped he understood. I'd needed to make the gesture.

"That's cool," he said. "Can we talk when you get back from Nationals?"

I nodded, not trusting myself to say anything else.

"Awesome," he said. "That way, I'll be able to say I'm hanging out with a national champion."

I lightly slapped his stomach, and even though I mostly got his shirt and barely tapped him, I still felt a small thrill. This was flirting! I was doing it! "Don't jinx me," I said.

"Impossible," he said, and I realized that even though David's teeth weren't as straight or white as Scott's, he had a very nice smile. Better, even, in some ways. When Scott looked at me, I thought about what an amazing person he was, but when David looked at me, it was like he was telling me how amazing *I* was. Maybe it was self-centered of me, but it felt good to be reminded of that once in a while.

I tried several times to connect with Christina, but it seemed like she was always busy collecting donations from people or showing them where to go. Finally, she came over to me. She had Lyla Quin with her.

"You remember Lyla, right?" Christina asked. I couldn't believe how casually she said the reporter's name, like they were bosom buddies.

"Of course," I said. "The interview you did was great." I figured this was not the time to mention that I hadn't seen it yet.

"I just want to do a follow-up," Lyla said, her

bright red lips stretching into a smile as she held out her hand. I shook it, feeling very grown-up.

"Thanks to Lyla, this fund-raiser's been a huge success," Christina said. "So far, we have more than enough to pay registration fees and the cost of your team leotard, warm-up suit, and duffel bag."

Lyla was smoothing her hair, although it didn't look any less poufy than when she'd first walked up. "Your friend is very enterprising."

Christina shrugged. "My publicity coach actually helped a lot," she said to me. "I asked her how I could get a good turnout for something like this, and she set up the thing with Channel Thirteen where they would advertise the event. Lyla said the station got a ton of e-mails from people wishing us all luck after her first interview, so people were eager to help you get to Nationals."

Lyla was gesturing now to her cameraman, the same guy who'd come out with her on her earlier visit to the gym. "I hate to rush y'all, but can I have you two move here? I want to get all the cars in the background, so we should get this shot while it's as busy as it is."

Christina and I moved to face the gym, the car wash at our backs. I realized I hadn't yet gotten to talk to Christina personally, which is what I really wanted to do, but Christina was already getting ready for the camera with her biggest smile and a toss of her hair.

Lyla nodded at the cameraman to begin rolling. "Well, y'all, we're back with our favorite local gymnasts." It was weird how she sounded the same, and yet different. It was like she took her normal voice but put this television spin on it that made it a little louder, her words enunciated more precisely. "Today we're at the Texas Twisters gym, where there's a car wash being held to raise money to send one promising gymnast to the Junior Nationals in a couple of weeks."

And even though I'd been expecting it, I still felt thrown off when Lyla actually turned to me. "Noelle, this fund-raiser is all for you. How does it feel to know you have so much community support?"

I tried to think about Christina's publicity coach, and the advice she might have given me on how to answer this question, but it all just flew out of my head. And I realized that I didn't need it. I knew exactly how to respond.

"It's awesome," I said. "I was having a hard time

believing in myself, and knowing that so many people believe in me . . . It really inspires me. You interviewed me before and asked me about gymnastics being such an individual sport, even though we may compete for our gym or our country. But I think this shows how team-oriented it is."

I was trying not to cry, because I didn't want to be a baby on television, but I had to clear my throat before I turned to Christina. "You're my best friend in the whole world," I said. "I can't thank you enough for all of this."

And then Christina was crying and hugging me, and I could feel the wetness in my own eyes, but I no longer cared about what anyone else might think. I was going to Junior Nationals, where I was going to do my absolute best to show everyone that their faith in me wasn't misplaced. I was going to travel to Philadelphia with the most incredible friends a girl could possibly ask for, and we were going to have the time of our lives. I'd woken up that morning feeling empty, and now my heart felt so full it could have burst.

Fifteen

Junior Nationals didn't go the way any of us had expected. Britt rolled her ankle on her floor routine on the first night of all-around competition and couldn't finish, which meant that she didn't qualify for event finals on one of her best events. Even though she taped up the ankle and was able to finish that night and the next, she wasn't in top form.

Christina fared a little better, placing ninth all around and qualifying for event finals on floor and bars. Finishing in the top ten meant that she had a chance to go to a camp that would help determine the final team of girls who'd compete in international competitions for the United States.

I'd be going with her to that camp, because I finished fifth all-around. Since the World team would consist of six members, as long as I proved myself to Coach Piserchia at the camp, I had a pretty good shot at making that team. I was still disappointed that I'd placed outside of the medals, but as David had pointed out in a congratulatory text message, it was pretty awesome to be one of the top five gymnasts in the country.

I really wished I had my own cell phone, so I wouldn't have to explain to my mother who it was that I kept texting back and forth. She'd teased me about it all through the team dinner we'd had the night before, which had turned out to be superdelicious Philly cheese steak sandwiches. Of course, Britt and Christina and I had eaten the meat and cheese without any bread, but they'd been tasty and not that expensive. Tomorrow, after the pressure of the competition was over, we were going to tour the historical parts of the city—where they had signed the Declaration of Independence and where Benjamin Franklin had lived, all for free or for a small donation. It was going to be so much fun.

* * *

Now it was the night of event finals. Britt had earned a silver on vault; Christina won a bronze on bars. It was my turn to go up on the beam.

I waited for the signal from the judges. Once the head judge lifted the green flag, I raised both my arms in a salute and forced myself to smile. Normally, I stayed pretty cool in competitions, but this time I knew the stakes were high and couldn't convince my body otherwise. This was the biggest competition of my life; I'd been through a lot to get here, and this was my last chance at a medal. My nerves were buzzing like a downed electrical wire.

I jumped into the first neckstand of my new mount, feeling my muscles stretch as I straddled my legs. Using my shoulders, I spun to face in the opposite direction, repeating the skill until it was like I was twirling around the beam, my legs scissoring straight and then straddling. I could hear a hush come over the audience, and I knew that this mount was something special. I wondered about my mother, sitting up in the stands and supporting me, and I hoped she knew that this mount was my way of saying I loved her. Every time I spun around that beam, the same way she'd done so many years ago, I was saying, *Thank you.*

I lowered myself to the beam and got to my feet, ready to launch right into my acrobatic series. The crucial part of the whole thing was making sure I connected the skills. I would earn bonus points on my score for starting my tumbling immediately after my feet came down from the handstand. Usually, it wasn't a problem; I'd been doing handstands on the beam since I was six years old, and keeping my balance was second nature. But on a stage this huge, you just never knew. Anything could happen.

But not this time. It was just like in practice. The balls of my feet touched down on the beam, and I barely felt my heels skim the surface as I threw my body backward into my first element: four layout-step-outs in a row, my feet coming down together squarely on the beam, one slightly in front of the other. Now this part was over, but I still had a little more than a minute left to go. When you're up there on that four-inch-wide beam, with the judges and thousands of spectators all watching you, a minute can feel like an eternity.

I had to get through a few dance elements and leaps before my next big skill, which included the mandatory full turn. Lifting one leg up until it was parallel to the beam, my toes pointed and my knee perfectly straight, I spun 360 degrees on the other foot. My heel came down hard on the beam as I stopped my momentum, but I didn't wobble. I allowed myself to let out a breath I hadn't even known I was holding.

Moves like that are sometimes more difficult than the really flashy ones. When you go to do something major on the beam, you prepare yourself for it. You slow down for just a second, square your shoulders, and imagine feeling your hands grabbing that beam the instant before it actually happens. If you make it, you feel energized. If you don't, you're disappointed in yourself, but at least you fall on something impressive.

But a full turn can be deceptive. It's relatively simple; it's something you've been doing since your compulsory routines in the lower levels. It's easy to rush through it, because you're already thinking ahead to the punch front with the blind landing you're about to do, or the illusion that's been giving you trouble in practice, where you keep kicking one leg up but can't get the complete circle you're supposed to get without touching your hand to the ground. If you make the full turn, you don't care.

Of course, you think. But if you don't make it, you suddenly find yourself standing on the mat with no idea how you got there. For the rest of the night, you think, *how could I have done that?*

The only big skill I had left before my dismount was a punch front, where I tucked my body into a front flip, the landing totally blind. I executed it cleanly, dancing my way to the end of the beam for my dismount.

This was it. I knew I'd had a good routine, and although I tried not to let myself think about the other gymnasts or the standings or the score, I couldn't help feeling hope blossom inside me while I stood there. My hands were rigid at my sides, my fingers pointed in toward my thighs as I touched my foot to the back of the beam, everything so familiar, even in this strange setting. And then I was launching myself into my round-off, and I knew I had the momentum. My back handspring was powerful, and I felt weightless as my feet left the beam for good. At that point, muscle memory took over, and I was spinning in the air, completing a full twist as my body spun in the first of two flips. And then my feet hit the mat.

It was a stuck landing. I threw my arms over my head in a salute, and this time I didn't have to force a smile. I knew it was one of the best routines I'd ever done.

Mo was waiting for me as I stepped down from the podium; she pressed me to her in a quick hug. It only lasted a second or two, but Mo rarely gave hugs, so I enjoyed the feeling of her hands squeezing my back, telling me before she even said the words that she was proud of me. "Good job," she said. "Good job."

Britt and Christina came to congratulate me, both wearing their warm-ups over their leotards. It was cold in the arena, and normally I would've put on my jacket immediately after finishing my routine, but my adrenaline was so high that I felt warm all over. Britt gave me a fist bump, and Christina wrapped one arm around me.

"You rocked it!" she said, and I put my arm around her waist to draw her closer.

"I couldn't have done it without you guys," I said, pulling Britt into a group hug.

And then came the hardest part: the waiting. Even though I'd had the routine of my life, there was a little voice inside telling me not to be too confident, that you never knew what the judges would do. It was possible they'd seen some minor bend of a knee here, or slight balance check there. Or maybe I hadn't connected two skills as fluidly as I needed to in order to get my bonus. Anything could happen.

Without having to search too hard, I found my family in the stands. I'd avoided glancing up at them too often during the competition, since I was worried that even a small wave from my brother or a smile from my mom would distract me. But now that it was all over, I allowed myself to look.

Only Mama and Mihai had been able to make the trip; it had been difficult enough to afford two extra tickets, much less the six that would have been needed to fly the whole family out.

I saw Mama standing up, clutching Mihai's hand in a tight grip, and I knew from the way her face looked all soft and shimmery that she was crying. Not in a sad way—more how she looked when the twins made her Mother's Day cards, or when Radu kissed her cheek in front of his friends. Mihai gave me a sheepish look like, *Sorry, you can't take her anywhere*, but he seemed different, too, as if he might explode from the force of his smile.

In that moment, I knew, even before they

flashed my score of 9.8. I knew it from the expressions on Mama's and Mihai's faces and the cheers of my teammates next to me. I'd won the gold medal. I was officially the best beam worker in the entire country, but even if I'd fallen, even if I'd gone home empty-handed, I knew that I still would've been the luckiest girl in the world.

Gymnastics glossary

acrobatic series: On the balance beam, at least three connected acrobatic or tumbling elements in a row from one end of the beam to the other

all-around competition: The part of a competition where gymnasts compete in all four events, and in which their combined scores are used to determine who is the best all-around athlete

Arabian: A skill where the gymnast jumps backward, as though to perform a backflip, then does a half twist in the air to execute a front flip, and lands facing forward. A *double Arabian* is a skill that involves two flips in the air instead of one.

beam: A horizontal, raised apparatus that is four inches wide, sixteen feet in length, and approximately four feet off the floor; on this, gymnasts perform a series of dance moves and acrobatic skills.

blind landing: A landing in which the gymnast ends up facing forward, sometimes away from the apparatus, and she cannot see the floor before landing

dance elements: Required dance sections of the routine that are done on the balance beam and used to connect acrobatic skills and leaps

difficulty level: A way of measuring what a skill is worth in the gymnastics code of points, or how hard a skill is to execute

event finals: The part of a competition during which the gymnasts with the highest preliminary scores on an apparatus compete to determine the best gymnast in each event

floor: A carpeted surface measuring forty feet square, over springs and wooden boards. Also the term for the only event in which a gymnast performs a routine set to music; the routine is ninety seconds in length, and composed of dance and acrobatic elements.

full-in: Two flips in the air with the first flip featuring a 360-degree twist

full turn: A 360-degree turn on one leg, performed on floor and beam

grips: Strip of leather placed on a gymnast's hand to prevent calluses and allow for a better grip on the uneven bars

handspring: A move in which a gymnast starts on both feet, jumps to a position supporting her body with just her two hands on the floor, and then pushes off to land on her feet again. This can be done forward or backward, and is typically used to start or connect an acrobatic series.

illusion: A turn requiring a lot of flexibility, starting with one leg high in the air; the gymnast swings her lifted leg in a circle, keeping her body in a straight position and creating the appearance of a front flip.

Junior Elite: The level before Senior Elite, as designated by regulations of the governing body of gymnastics. Junior Elite gymnasts are not allowed to compete in the Olympics.

layout: A maneuver completed in the air with hands held against the body and a pencil-straight overall position; flipping can be forward or backward, and the move ends with the gymnast standing on both feet again.

parallel bars: One of six apparatuses in men's artistic gymnastics. The parallel bars are much like the women's uneven bars in that there are two bars, but instead of one being high and one being low, they are at the same height and closer together.

pike: A position in which the body is bent double at the hips, with legs straight and toes pointed

pommel horse: One of six apparatuses in men's artistic gymnastics. The pommel horse is a padded, nearly cylindrical apparatus similar to the old-fashioned vaulting horse, which has two graspable pommels on top. The gymnast performs a series of balancing, swinging, and rotating maneuvers to earn his score.

press handstand: A move beginning on the floor with legs in a straddle position and all of the weight on the hands. The entire body is raised over the head and moves from a straddle position into a straight-body handstand.

punch front: A jump from a position on both feet into a forward-flipping somersault in which the gymnast lands again on both feet, still facing forward

release skill: Any skill performed on the uneven bars that requires the gymnast's hands to leave the bar before returning to it, usually after a twisting or flipping skill has been executed

round-off: A move that begins like a cartwheel, but

in which the legs swing together overhead, and the gymnast finishes facing in the opposite direction

Senior Elite: The level after Junior Elite, as designated by regulations of the governing body of gymnastics. In women's artistic gymnastics, a gymnast must be turning sixteen years of age within the calendar year during which the competition takes place to become a Senior Elite.

split: A position in which one leg is stretched in front of the body and the other behind

still rings: One of the six apparatuses in men's artistic gymnastics. Two rings are suspended from cables, and the gymnast must use them to perform a series of strength maneuvers, holding himself high off the ground, while controlling the movement of the rings, which are meant to remain as still as possible.

straddle: A position in which the right leg is stretched out to the right side of the body and the left leg is stretched out to the left, as the gymnast faces forward

stuck dismount: A move in which a gymnast executes a landing with both feet firmly planted on the ground and no wobbling occurs

tuck: A position in which the knees are folded in toward the chest at a ninety-degree angle, with the waist bent, creating the shape of a ball

tumbling passes: A series of connected acrobatic moves required in a floor-exercise routine

twist: A rotation of the body around the horizontal and vertical axis. Twisting is completed when a gymnast is flipping simultaneously, performing both actions at the same time in the same element. Twisting elements are typically named for the number of rotations completed (e.g.: a half twist is 180 degrees, or half a rotation; a full twist is 360 degrees, or a full rotation; and a double twist is 720 degrees, or two complete rotations).

uneven bars: (often, just "bars") One of four apparatuses in women's artistic gymnastics. Bars features the apparatus on which women perform mostly using their upper-body strength. This event consists of two rails placed at an uneven level; one bar acts as the high bar and the other as the low bar. Both bars are flexible, helping the gymnast to connect skills from one to the other.

vault: A runway of approximately eighty feet in length, leading to a springboard and a padded table at one end. The gymnast runs full speed toward the table, using the springboard to launch herself onto it; she then pushes off with her hands, moving into a series of flips and/or twists before landing on the mat behind the table.

walkover: A basic gymnastics skill where the gymnast either arches backward (for a back walkover) or leans forward (for a front walkover), places her hands on the mat to lift herself into a handstand, and holds a split position before "walking" each foot back to the ground

Yurchenko vault: A vaulting move that begins with a round-off onto the springboard, followed by a back handspring onto the table; the gymnast then pushes off into a series of flips and/or twists before landing on the mat. This style vault was named after Soviet gymnast Natalia Yurchenko.